HALLELUJAH I'M A BUM

A Novel

ROGER QUAM

Copyright © 2016 by Roger Quam

Hallelujah I'm a Bum
by Roger Quam

Printed in the United States of America.

ISBN 9781498478199

All rights reserved solely by the author. The author guarantees all contents are original and do not infringe upon the legal rights of any other person or work. No part of this book may be reproduced in any form without the permission of the author. The views expressed in this book are not necessarily those of the publisher.

Unless otherwise indicated, Scripture quotations taken from the New King James Version (NKJV). Copyright © 1982 by Thomas Nelson, Inc. Used by permission. All rights reserved.

www.xulonpress.com

Preface

In order to build tanks, ships, planes, and weapons during WW 2, it required massive amounts of metal and various other materials. A single tank needed 18 tons of metal, and one of the navy's biggest ships took 900 tons. Anything using scrap metal — from chicken wire to grain binders were needed to win the war. Commodities from sugar to gasoline were rationed. Americans were urged to turn in scrap metal for recycling, and schools and community groups across the country held scrap drives. The war caused the USA to be short of many materials. Counties across the United States organized scrap drives and collected old machinery, old rags, scrap newspaper, cattle bones, animal fat, and dozens of other items. One scrap drive produced a 5-gallon pail of old razor blades—one of many unusual scrap collection stories. This effort came on the heels of the Great Depression which saw many men, women, and young people walking the highways and riding the railroads looking for jobs, food, shelter, and clothes. In a few instances some families sent their children down the road in order to increase their chances for survival. In other words, the mothers and dads let their sons become hobos, tramps, bums, or whatever people called them at that time.

I was raised by a father who was in the scrap metal and fur business and was involved in a county salvage program. We also lived less than 200 feet from the main line of the Northern Pacific Railroad. We were able to view the tanks, Jeeps, trucks, troop trains, and multitude of tramps riding in boxcars as they rolled past.

Roger Quam, Born in 1940 and raised in Hawley, Minnesota.

CHAPTER 1

June 26, 1942

It was on a beautiful sunny California Sunday afternoon when 17 year old George Robinson's parents took him down to the local railroad yard and proceeded to bid him farewell on a slow moving freight. He and his parents had talked about what was about to happen for the past several weeks, but now it was about to happen. Other families in their neighborhood were in a similar boat—not able to survive the depression with little work, insufficient food, lack of money to buy clothes, and very little hope. In George's situation it was also his ethnicity that was the issue—he was the son of a Japanese father and an American mother.

With the bombing of Pearl Harbor and the United States declaration of war on Japan, many of the Japanese were being interned in camps in various parts of the west coast. George's parents had met in Japan when his mother was a missionary in the 1920s. George was born in Tokyo and brought to America along with his sister. A brother was born in the suburb of Los Angeles, thus making it a family of five. At this time, the geo-political situation for anyone even part Japanese made living anywhere on the west coast region very difficult. George understood the problem and determined that running away would be best for both himself and his family.

George was over 6 feet tall, unlike most Japanese boys his age, probably due to the fact that his mother was tall and Swedish. He had black hair, large hands, and was a good athlete. Their entire family was of the Christian religion.

They had just attended Sunday school and the Sunday morning church service with their three children at the Japanese Bible church. His mother had packed a lunch for George—cheese sandwiches, a container of cooked rice, several cookies, pickles, and an apple. There was also a 2-quart jar filled with ice cubes and water. His mother, Veronica, insulated the jar well by wrapping it in newspaper and placing it in a heavy sugar sack. Those provisions would provide him sustenance until the train took him out of the suburbs of the Los Angeles area. It would be up to him to find some additional food and water for the remainder of the trip. George had about 20 dollars in cash and change that he had saved up from odd jobs where he had worked the first part of the summer.

"No sense in prolonging our goodbyes, so let's get on with it," the father said. The mother, face wet with tears, stood in silence as a slow moving freight train rolled through the railyard. "George, let me briefly pray before you climb on," his father said.

"OK, dad," George responded. His mother joined him and his dad with their hands as the 3 steam engines rolled slowly by them. As his father began to speak, they moved their heads close together so they could hear him pray.

> *"Lord, provide guardian angels for our son and help him find his way. You have some divine plan for him*

Chapter 1

---

and he will do your will. Let us meet again someday, if not in this world, in the next. We place him into your all-powerful guiding hands.—Amen."

George grabbed onto a boxcar ladder, then onto a small platform, and was soon out of sight as the train picked up speed and he quickly disappeared. The last thing his mom and dad saw was his backpack as the railcars rounded the curve.

George's family lived only two blocks from the rail yards where many of his Japanese friends would watch the trains as they did their switching every day. They also spent time observing the men, and some children and women as they used the open boxcars to ride in.

The train soon slowed up and stopped to change tracks. George quickly jumped off from where he was standing and found an open boxcar. He climbed in and joined with a group of individuals who had the same idea he had. He had heard stories about the characters who frequented these boxcars. He was now face to face with them.

1500 miles east of California was the small town of Harriet, Wisconsin—population 1822. It was the home of Thomas and Mildred Olson and their 16 year old daughter, Wanda. Thomas was a farmer who had gone bankrupt during the early 1930s, lost his farm, and was barely surviving on his new business venture of scrap iron and metal. He also worked at odd jobs during the winter months and made extra cash by trapping fur-bearing animals. Mr. Olson was from Swedish ancestors and his wife Mildred of 18 years came from Norwegian roots and was a very talented homemaker.

Their daughter was a very beautiful young woman who was about to enter her senior year in high school. She was not a happy person in the current situation with there not being adequate finances to support the family like the daughter wished. Most of Wanda's friends were in the same boat as she was from relatively poor families who had also gone through the depression.

There was the normal amount of peer pressure among the girls in her class. They all wanted the latest styles in clothes that their parents could not afford. Of the 34 students in her class, 20 of them were girls. Most of the girls longed for the time when they would finally graduate and be free to escape the small town where they felt trapped. A couple of them had family finances sufficient to attend college when they were finished with high school. Wanda had high grades and was hoping she could qualify for a nursing scholarship when she graduated.

Most of the mothers sewed their daughter's dresses, shirts, and skirts from designer flour and feed sack materials. Those girls whose parents could afford better clothes had a belittling name for the flour sack print clothes—they called them "feed apparel." Although some of the girls felt inferior by wearing the feed apparel, their mothers took pride in entering many of their creations in the county fair. The fair board had special categories with many prizes. Mrs. Olson had won many prizes over the years. There was also a category for old antiques that were made into lamps.

On this particular day Wanda's mother asked her to walk uptown to the store and get some coffee and bread before the noon meal. "See

Chapter 1

how fresh the hamburger buns are while you are there. We will need some for tomorrow. It's the 4th of July in a few days, you know. Find out what time today they will have fresh buns delivered from the bakery. I may have to send you back later to pick up some."

"Do I have them place the charges on our bill?" Wanda asked her mother. "Also, Mom, can I get some red thread so you can finish my new dress?"

"Yes, and tell Ted that I will be in on Friday to pay up to date whatever we owe. Be sure that you take the bat with you. You never know what some of those homeless guys along the tracks may have on their minds, and I think you know what I am talking about — especially when they are drunk."

Within 15 minutes Wanda was on her way to the downtown grocery store, walking along the Chicago and Northwestern Railroad tracks. She had a cloth bag in one hand, and a sawed off baseball bat in the other. She never had to use the bat on any of the transients along the track. However, she did have to use it to scare off some of the animals and dogs a couple of times.

As Wanda walked along the tracks she waved at several mothers of friends who were in backyards working on mowing lawns, weeding gardens, or hanging up clothes. Wanda knew all of them by name. Harriet was a typical friendly, yet gossipy small town.

Maud Jacobson had her entire wash of white clothes ruined yesterday when the #323 came through just after 9 a.m. with the steam engine belting out great volumes of thick coal black smoke. Normally, the smoke would rise up high in the sky quickly and wouldn't bother the clothes. Yesterday morning, because of the atmosphere, the smoke from the engine's fire box, hung along just above the ground almost all the way through town, ruining her entire weekly wash. Maud was as mad as could be. She complained to the Railroad officials at the depot, but received no compassion or apology.

As Wanda walked along she could see that there were houses where a few of the young and even middle aged men were missing and gone off to war. It was the same situation all over the United States. Because of Thomas' role in the scrap steel and metal business he was able to evade being drafted into the wars. His role in the next four years would be of utmost importance in the war effort.

The war in the pacific and in Europe had taken many of the young men away from Harriet and from the young women who knew them all. It also took away the available labor pool for Harriet's commerce and the agriculture industry. Thomas was especially hit hard by the labor shortage for his scrap metal business. At this time Thomas was the only employee in the business—himself. He had even thought about employing some of the women in Harriet.

Back on the west coast, George had survived his first night on the slow moving freight. The food and water that his mother had provided for him at the start was almost all gone. The first day was very hot and standing inside the boxcar made it that much hotter. The people he met on the train that first day were a good mixture of what he was to experience during the next few days—people with no hope for the present and little hope for the future.

A group of workers had apparently just been paid by their farm employer. One of the men had been seen by the others counting his money—something that, George learned quickly, was never to be done in a railroad boxcar. After the guy put his stash of bills back

Chapter 1

into his suitcase, a big strong guy grabbed him and threw him out of the open boxcar door and onto the track. Then he opened his suitcase, took out the guy's money, put it in his own pocket, and threw the suitcase out onto the tracks. George knew that the man was surely injured, even killed. *What should I do? I cannot just leave him on the tracks?*—was his thought.

While the other guys turned their faces, George grabbed his own bag and jumped off of the train which by this time had slowed to a crawl waiting to take its turn on the east coast bound set of tracks. He walked back a couple blocks and found the elderly man lying on one of the rails. He was unconscious and bleeding from his nose and arm. George picked him up and carried him over under a shady tree out of the hot sun. *I need to give him first aid*, he thought. *But I don't have any first aid supplies.* He took what little water he had left and cleaned the blood off of his wounds using a clean white shirt his mother had packed for him. Once he stopped the bleeding, he wrapped the wounds with two of his clean white handkerchiefs.

George spotted a little white house some 500 feet from the track and decided to take a chance of finding someone home that could provide some comfort and rest for the poor old man. He carried the man to the doorstep of the house and set him gently down. He knocked with his right fist. Soon an elderly woman appeared in the doorway. "Can I help you sir," she asked. "Oh, my goodness! What happened to that poor man?

"This man has been injured and needs some medical attention and rest," George said. "I found him on the tracks. Can you help him?"

"Yes I can and will help him," the woman answered in a kind manner. "Bring him into my guest room." By this time the man was semiconscious and wanting some water. The nice lady brought a glass of cold water and George helped him to drink it.

George returned back to the tracks, retrieved the man's suitcase, clothes, and gave it back to him at the nice lady's house.

Back in 1936—Harriet, Wis.

Thomas Olson had started the Olson Scrap Iron and Metal Company on January 1, 1936. He had lost his parent's farm which he inherited during the 1930s and was now living on his wife's parent's inheritance money and their property along the railroad tracts. The money problems that existed in the Olson family had caused Thomas and Mildred to become closer to each other. It did have a different effect on Wanda. She wanted to escape from home as soon as she graduated from high school.

Thomas had noticed that all of the farms in and around Harriet had accumulated a mountain of old farm machinery. Most of the machinery was of the horse drawn type, as the tractor drawn type had not filtered into the countryside as yet—especially after the 1929 depression and the resultant bank failures. Many farmers could barely afford replacement parts for their existing equipment.

During the spring of 1938 Thomas was eating at Ginny's Café on the main street of Harriet. A man came into the café and ordered a chicken chow Mein dinner and a pot of tea. Because the café happened to be crowded at that time of day, Thomas offered to share his booth with the man. The man was Japanese but spoke good English. Most residents of Harriet were ignorant of anything Japanese, being mostly Norwegian, Swedish, Danish, and German. However, from the reaction of the occupants in the café who saw that the man was looking for a place to sit, one could plainly see that there was no lack of prejudice feeling toward the man. A brother of Thomas' who was

Chapter 1

an English teacher in Japan in the 1920s had familiarized him with the Japanese people and culture. Thomas had long been convinced that they were good people.

The man, whose name Tsug Eniles was printed on his business case, thanked Thomas with a bow, and sat down in his booth. "My name Tsug. Your name?"

"My name is Thomas Olson and I live in this town," he answered politely.

"Harriet town?" Tsug asked.

"Yes Harriet town," George responded with a smile. "What are you in Harriet for—what business?" Thomas was not quite sure what a Japanese businessman would be doing in Harriet, Wisconsin. *Probably trying to find some grain sources and make out some contracts,* he thought to himself. He had studied and read where the Japanese needed enormous quantities of food to feed its millions of people. Japan was also in a war with some of its neighboring countries at that time.

"I work for a Japanese Company that makes farm equipment. I am looking for a good source of #1 and #2 scrap steel that can be used to make Japanese farm machinery. I need to find some scrap iron dealers. Might you know of someone who could help me?" Thomas sat in silence for a period of 10 seconds. He wasn't quite sure if he had heard his booth partner correctly.

"Has someone been talking to you about me," George replied, "did someone tell you that I was in the scrap iron business?"

"You are the only person I have ever met from Harriett town. We did know that there was a mountain of steel machinery lying in the farmyards and fields in and around Wisconsin."

"How did you know that fact?" Thomas asked.

"My Company took some aerial photos using a high altitude special camera," the man from Japan answered.

"Well Tsug, I am a Christian and I pray every morning that God will guide my paths. I believe that my paths led me into your paths this morning," Thomas said, not knowing if his new friend understood fully what he was talking about. "Let me ask you this question: If I could guarantee a certain amount of scrap steel in one year, how would we ship it and how much would you pay for it?"

"Can I call you Thomas?" Tsug asked.

"I wish you would," Thomas answered.

"Let me think about it and let's meet again tomorrow for breakfast Mr. Thomas."

"I'll be here at 7 a.m.," Thomas responded.

The next morning Thomas went to the same café an hour before Tsug arrived. He wanted to write out a business plan for expanding an anticipated increase if he were to clean up much of the scrap machinery in the 10 mile radius around Harriet. He would need at least one truck, a car with trailer hitch, a 1 ton trailer, an acetylene cutting torch, some miscellaneous tools, a boom wrecker, improvement on the rail siding loading platform, and at least one or two additional persons for labor.

The railroad would take care of improvements on the loading platform, the equipment could be purchased or built locally, and the land needed Thomas already had in his procession. The problem would be the labor needed. He would need to pray for all of the pieces

Chapter 1

of the proposed business expansion plan to be somehow provided. This would include a loan from the bank for cash flow.

While he was sitting in the booth, the café owner walked up to Thomas and sat down across from him. He began speaking to him, "I hope you do not have that foreign guy at your booth again this morning. We had several complaints after you and he were sitting here yesterday."

"Is that so? And who were the complainers?" Thomas asked.

"I would rather not say." the manager answered.

"Well then, I will not talk to you about providing the dinner for our next catered Saturday Church meal for 100 people. How does that grab you? Put that in your pipe and smoke it." The manager just sat there and was completely silenced.

"I will talk to those racist numbskulls. Go ahead and invite your friend in to eat with you." Just then the Japanese fellow walked in. He sat down where the manager had just gotten up and walked away.

"Good morning Thomas, did you have a good sleep?" he said with a bright smile.

"I did Tsug, and I am all set for us to do business," was the reaction from the Harriet scrap dealer. "Let's first order breakfast. I'm going to have their good wheat pancakes and sausage."

"Wheat Pancakes and sausage for me too," the Japanese businessman agreed. "What did you come up with?"

"I drove at least 100 miles yesterday afternoon and night and viewed much of the old machinery hidden in the farms and woods. You cannot believe how much steel is out there, most of it hidden in the weeds—mowers, grain binders, potato planters and diggers, hay balers, threshing machines, old cars—all sitting and rusting in the fields and woods."

"What would be your best estimate as to how much?" Tsug asked.

"Assuming we could work from May 1 to September 30, have all the labor we needed, and not have the winter snow interrupt us too much, we could ship out 1 carload of scrap per week. That would be 21 carloads in 5 months—or 1,575,000 pounds."

"That would be great and my company in Japan would be very happy. I will contact them and make up a contract for $8 a ton for #1 steel, $7 a ton for #2 steel and $12 a ton for good clean cast iron. We can also advance you money so you can pay your customers a fair price and buy some needed equipment. The steel would be shipped F.O.B. (Free on board)—Harriet."

When they were finished, Tsug got up and walked toward the kitchen where he found the cook. "I ate some of your chicken chow mein last night. Tell me, do you make your own chow mein or do you buy it ready-made? It tastes better than my mother's back in Japan." He then left the kitchen cook a nice tip after receiving a copy of the cook's chow mein recipe.

In the next five years, from 1936 to 1941, the Olson Scrap Iron and Metal Company shipped out old obsolete and scrap farm machinery from a radius of 30 miles around Harriet. Almost all of the scrap iron was shipped to Japan. Much of all labor was provided by some of the farmers and their high school sons. Many of them wanted to work as many hours as possible. Some of them would start as early as 5 am, or when the sun provided enough light so they could see what they were doing. Many would work until dark. The high school football coach worked with Thomas in having his players use the loading of

Chapter 1

rail cars as a means of building up their bodies with powerful muscles. When it came to potato picking time, the high school girls took over that job. As long as the snow didn't cover the scrap iron, the business kept going into the fall and started early in the spring.

Back to 1942

Thomas' and Mildred's daughter, Wanda was becoming a tall beautiful young woman. Her beauty was beginning to worry both Thomas and Mildred as she was becoming more and more popular with the boys in her class. Another worry they had was the neighborhood in which they lived. It was on the edge of town and near one of the most popular hobo-towns in the U.S. Most freight trains had a multitude of free riders on every train. The Thomas's viewed these men as potential predators of their daughter. They would talk about it very often and wondered how to handle it. The best thing they could come up with was to require Wanda to observe strict hours and keep their main gate locked at night.

Wanda worked at some of the least messy jobs in the scrap metal business for her dad. She would write out checks for scrap bought from customers when it was handy or when Mr. and Mrs. Olson were gone. The business bought wool from sheep ranchers and shipped it to a co-op distribution point in Saint Paul. Wanda was able to handle this task as long as she had someone else handle the heavy wool sacks—some of which weighed 150-250 pounds.

The church that the family attended was a bible believing and teaching church with 65 people in attendance. Wanda was involved with the Youth of the church and the mission group. When she was a junior in the summer of 1941, their Youth group traveled to Ethiopia on a mission trip and helped build a church in the center of the city of Addis Ababa.

Thomas and Mildred were members of the local Business Commerce Club, joining in 1941. Their reason for joining was to combat any further criticism of Thomas' participation in selling scrap iron to Japan in the late 1930s. It was on purpose that he joined. He did not know that the Japanese were using the scrap to make war equipment. It was explained very clearly to the chamber and most of the members accepted Thomas' explanation. Both Thomas and Mildred were very active in community activities and more than made up for what was perceived as doing something wrong to the country.

Thomas was beginning to understand what was going on with the international scene. He could sense that a world war was making its way toward the United States. Nothing about it could be good for anyone. Mad men were loose in the world—one in Germany, one in Japan, and one in Italy.

Chapter 2

July 2, 1942

Mildred Olson was outside early on a Friday morning when she all of a sudden spotted what looked like a body lying in the section of tall grass that her husband had not had time to mow the day before. She didn't know if the body was alive or dead. Since the depression, many men and an occasional woman were found along the railroad tracks sleeping in the nice soft green grass on the Olson lawn. Sometimes the men and women were slightly drunk with the cheap liquor that they could afford and had acquired. There were a couple occasions when a lifeless body was found along the tracks from one of several causes of death. Mildred walked over to the body and touched the foot with her shoe. The person moved slightly and then jumped up! His sudden motion suddenly scared Mildred and she stepped backwards quickly.

"Oh," he said with an apologetic tone in his voice, "I never meant to scare you. I will get off your property. I am just passing through and looking for work. Do you happen to know where there may be an opening for some work?" By this time he was on his feet with his shoes back on. They both walked toward the front door.

"What kind of work do you want?" Mildred asked. "What is your name?"

"I can do most anything—anything requiring physical labor. My name is George."

"Let me ask my husband." Mildred opened the kitchen door and yelled inside to her husband, "Thomas, do you know of anyone who could use some help right now?"

"Who is asking?" the voice answered from inside the house.

"This young fellow who just spent the night sleeping on our front lawn. What is your name again, young man?" Mildred asked. Thomas, her husband, was on the front porch within a few seconds.

"Young man, have you ever loaded scrap iron into a gondola car?" Thomas asked George.

"No sir, I have not, but I'll bet it wouldn't take me more than a few minutes to learn." At this point Mildred stepped out of the kitchen once again and faced the young man that she was already beginning to become fond of. She saw in him the young man like the son that Thomas and she had lost early in their marriage when he was only 6.

"What is your name young man?" she repeated her question once more.

"My name is George, ma'am."

"Why don't you go to our bathroom, George, wash up, and come and eat breakfast with us," Mildred said.

"I can eat outside if you want," he responded, "I'm a little dirty from my ride on the train."

"No Son, we would be honored to have you as our guest. Just walk down the hall to the second door on the left," Mildred requested once again. "You will find the bathroom." He left the kitchen and walked to the second door down the hall. He walked into a neatly

Chapter 2

kept bathroom. George felt unclean compared to this clean bathroom. When he was done washing up he started back to the kitchen table.

Just as he came back to the kitchen from the bathroom, Mildred's 17 year old daughter Wanda walked down from her upstairs bedroom.

"Good morning, Wanda," Mildred greeted her daughter. She sensed that Wanda was not in the greatest of moods, at least not her best mood. Imagine the surprise and questions in Wanda's mind when the uninvited guest walked back to the table from the bathroom and sat down. Both Wanda and George just stared at each other.

Wanda then looked at her mother. George acted polite and said, "Hello, my name is George." Mildred needed to quickly explain to Wanda the incursion into their breakfast table.

"Wanda," Mildred said to her daughter, "George here was found by me, early this morning, sleeping on our lawn by the railroad track after having traveled in on the morning freight. He looked tired and hungry so I invited him for breakfast. Your father is thinking about hiring him to work in the scrapyard." It was then that Mildred noticed that George had cleaned himself up to the point where his washed face and arms now revealed that he was most likely from the orient. Mildred guessed Japan.

"Ma'am," George spoke to Mildred, "I would have taken my shoes off outside, but one of the men on the freight stole the socks out of my backpack. I have no clean socks."

"That is quite all right, you may wear your shoes in our house," his host answered.

"Well, that's really nice," Wanda replied with an unsympathetic and sarcastic tone.

"So, Wanda," George said in a pleasant voice, "what year are you in school?" There was a pause.

"I don't think that should be of any particular concern of yours," Wanda answered with an increasingly conceited response. George immediately dropped the subject, knowing that any further comment would just irritate her more. He folded his hands and quietly said the table grace, thinking that Mildred had not already voiced the mealtime prayer. Both Wanda and Mildred noticed George praying. Then he began to eat. His hunger could not keep him from wolfing his food down.

"Ma'am, I apologize for my manners this morning. I am so hungry and this breakfast makes me think that I have died and gone to heaven. It's the first time I have eaten since last Sunday night."

"You're kidding me George," Mildred replied, "you haven't eaten for four days?"

"That's correct ma'am." George looked over at Wanda. She was getting bored. There was not a care in her face.

Mildred needed to know more about George's background. Her husband had trouble hiring good workers in his business and especially honest ones. The War in Europe and the Pacific had taken most of the young workers in Harriet to fight. Even some of the middle aged men were enlisting. *George looked honest and would make a good worker*, Mildred thought to herself. "George, have some more eggs and bacon. I will make some more toast. Eat as much as you want and then we will talk about you. I would like to know where you are from, about your family, your schooling, etc." Wanda suddenly stood up and excused herself from the table.

"I need to run over to the school this morning to register for the fall semester," she said to her mother. "I should be home by 10 a.m. If Bruce calls, tell him I will see him tonight when we go to the movie."

Chapter 2

"Goodbye, Wanda," George said as she walked out of the room. Wanda did not respond to him.

Thomas and Mildred were together for morning coffee and were discussing George and how he would be housed if he was going to work in the scrap business. "Tom," Mildred started out, "George has no money, no work clothes and he needs to have a place to sleep. How about if we let him sleep in the equipment shed next to the railroad track? It will be a little noisy but he will soon get used to it. He is probably accustomed to the noise of trains."

"That should be OK Mildred," Thomas commented, "I just do not want him sleeping close to Wanda's room since we do not know him that well. Maybe later on if his employment works out and he stays longer than a few weeks, we can have him sleep in the downstairs storeroom, especially as it gets closer to winter. I will have Wanda clean the equipment shed tomorrow. Until then, he will have to sleep in a sleeping bag on the couch. It may be risky in hiring him. We have no background information on him and he could be a criminal. But, I have to have someone to do the work for me and I have no choice."

"You may be interested in the fact that he prayed at the table before he ate. He is probably Christian. Also, have you noticed that George looks Japanese or Chinese?" Mildred asked.

"Yes I did notice, but not until he had cleaned off his face," Thomas replied. "He must have been in line from the steam engine smoke directly into the boxcar."

"If he is Japanese, will it get us into trouble? Is that going to be a problem if he goes to work for you?" Mildred asked. "You know how sensitive this country is about the Japanese right now." Thomas took another sip of his coffee and a bite from the cookie he was working on.

"We may have some trouble since they are rounding up many of the Japanese on the west coast and interning them into camps in various places."

"Maybe we will get into trouble if you hire him in your business." Mildred responded.

"Not in Harriet, Wisconsin, especially with the labor shortage," Thomas answered. "We will just need to keep him away from the downtown nightlife. His appearance could start a riot, maybe."

That morning Thomas began immediately to teach George about the scrap business. "Let's take a walk out to the scrap yard. I will show you some of what the scrap business is all about."

"What I will do is to pay you $.50 per hour for the first 3 months. After that, I will pay you $1.00 per hour. Here is the catch—and it is a good one—you can put in as many hours as you wish. We will also feed you and buy you clothes. Does that sound ok?"

"Sounds great, Mr. Olson," George responded.

"Now," Mr. Olson said, "the first thing you need to know is the size of the steel that is ready to be placed directly into steel mill hoppers. The size is 36 inches long by 18 inches wide. To make it easy, I think of the size as being from the ground up to my hip for the 36 inches and from my elbow up to the end of my fingers for the 18 inches. Using this method of measuring you don't have to use a tape measure or yard stick. Every once in a while take a yard stick and

Chapter 2

see where 36 inches reaches from the ground up on your pants leg. See how close you are."

"Does that go for all steel, Mr. Olson?" George was asking the questions that Thomas hoped he would. It showed that he was taking an interest in what Thomas was telling him.

"Any cast iron has to be separated from the steel. Cast iron is made of material that is easy to break with a hammer or sledge hammer. It also is very difficult to cut with a cutting torch. On this hay mower, for example, try breaking this cast iron hub off of this steel shaft," challenged Thomas. With one crack of the sledge hammer, George broke off the cast iron.

"That was easy," was George's response.

"Now, George, let's teach you how to use the cutting torch." George was very eager to learn all the ins and outs of working in a scrap yard. "This is the torch head. Turn this knob about a half a turn, light the tip with the lighter, and adjust the second knob until 4 even flames come out the tip. Heat the steel that you wish to cut until it is almost red hot. Then pull the trigger and move the end of the flame as the molten steel is sent to the ground." Try to position the tip so that the molten steel all goes to the ground.

After a two hour session, they concluded by having an ice cold bottle of homemade root beer. On their way back to the house Thomas remarked, "George, you are a natural at working with scrap iron. I need to keep you. I just hope the U.S. Army doesn't come and enlist you."

"They won't," George replied. "I wanted to enlist back in California, but I guess my nationality prevented me from joining."

"One of your parents is Japanese—is that correct?" Thomas asked. "Are they going to intern your family in one of those camps?"

"I suspect that they are, if they haven't already." George answered. "I never stuck around to find out. I really do not dare to write and find out. If they found out that I was here they would come and get me—maybe with guns."

"Well, let's hope not," Thomas responded. "OK, let me show you next how to operate the scale. A customer will drive onto the scale with a load of scrap iron. Make sure that the car and trailer, or pickup is completely on the scale. Record the weight, which will be the gross weight. When the customer and you, or the customer alone is done unloading the scrap, he will once more drive onto the scale. That weight is the tare weight. The difference between the two weights is the net weight. Watch for the customer attempting to cheat in some manner. Just keep your eyes peeled for some shady practices. Just remember that not all of the people are honest. We use our kitchen as an office and there is where the customer will get paid for his scrap iron.

"There is one other item I need to talk to you about. It involves our daughter. She is at that age when boys and even some men are interested in her beauty. Do you know what I am talking about, George?"

"I do. I wasn't born yesterday," George answered in a manner that indicated he knew what Thomas was talking about.

"What I am worried about is all of the men walking the tracks and riding in boxcars. I am afraid that something may happen to her from those men. What I would like you to do is to be her behind the scenes

Chapter 2

body guard. Do you think that you can do that?" Thomas was taking a huge risk in asking George to do this. But he had no one else to ask.

"Thomas, I have had the same thoughts about those guys riding the trains. I will do that for you. I would suggest that we put up a street light at the gate into the property. Your place was dark when I got here this morning. This will provide some protection for both Mildred and Wanda when they drive in at night. Does Wanda drive yet?"

"No, she doesn't, but she is going to take a driving course at school sometime this year. It's something new that the school is offering this fall. By the way, do not tell Mildred that we had this talk."

"You've got it Mr. Olson," George said.

"Oh, one other thing, George." You may need to train in some other new workers from time to time, just like I have trained you.

Soon Wanda returned from her school and met her mother in the kitchen. "Wanda," she said, "I have a job for you. It will take you most of the day tomorrow."

"What is the job mom, I hope it doesn't take too long."

"Dad and I need to have you clean out the machine shed next to the railroad tracks so George can stay in it, at least temporarily. He is a God-send to us as a worker. Maybe I will ask George to help you." At that moment, George walked into the kitchen from the living room and then outside to escape the discussion concerning him. As soon as the kitchen door was shut, Wanda turned to her mother and spoke.

"Does he have to stay with us, Mom? I don't like him." she complained.

"So what is wrong with him, what don't you like about him?"

"He seems really creepy, Mom," Wanda answered. "He's unshaven, his clothes smell, his clothes have holes in them, and he probably hasn't been to more than the 8th grade in education. I think he is a bum, just like the tramps and hobos you and Dad are always telling me to watch out for." Wanda's mother sat down at the kitchen table, took a sheet of white paper, a pencil, and wrote on the top of it: <u>For George</u>– She looked at her daughter and fixed her eyes directly into hers.

"Wanda, do you remember what our sermon was about last Sunday that Pastor Williams delivered to us?"

"I do not remember, Mother," Wanda answered. "I sometimes have trouble remembering what you served at your last meal. Remind me."

"Try the Parable of the Good Samaritan," Mildred responded.

"You are so correct, Mother," she answered. "I remember the title, but I slept through most of the sermon."

"So, let's see, you say that George needs a good shave, maybe even a haircut." Mildred wrote 'haircut and shave' on the piece of paper. "What else?"

"His clothes smell and they have holes in them," Wanda repeated.

"So they need washing and mending," her mother answered back. "I'll write those down on the list."

"Mom, I get the idea," Wanda's voice rose slightly.

'Here Wanda, you finish the list. It will be your homework for Sunday school. Once you finish the list, you can start to fulfill the list by collecting the items for George."

"But Mom," Wanda began to protest, "we don't have Sunday school for another 2 ½ months. I realize that you are the high school age Sunday school teacher during the rest of the year, but the Sunday school takes a vacation in the summer time."

Chapter 2

"Not this summer," her mother answered, "at least not for you and for the next few days. This will be a chance for you to put your faith into action."

"Let me tell you Mom, I don't agree with this," Wanda protested again.

"Don't agree with what?" Her mother replied.

"The list that we are making and what you are concluding—what I am to do with the list."

"Look, Wanda, I don't want you to do this, other than to clean up the tool shed and find some items that George needs. What I do want is for you to <u>want</u> to do this." Wanda stood up, took the paper and pencil, walked into the living room and sat down on her favorite chair. She had just been convicted of not wanting to do something that she knew was right to do. Along with the pastor's sermon on the Good Samaritan was the scripture that said, 'if you know something is right to do, and you refuse to do it, you are sinning.'

Wanda continued her Good Samaritan list for George. The list included: 2 bars of soap, 3 pairs of socks, Sunday dress shoes, a Sunday suit, 2 ties, pairs of undershorts, t-shirts, dress shirts, work clothes, work boots, work gloves, shaving supplies, and some miscellaneous other clothes and supplies. Now she wondered how she was going to fill the list. The only place she could think of was their church basement 'poor room.' Maybe she could also spread the word to the Missionary Circle Group of this need. Of course, George needed to try on some of the clothes to make sure that they all fit him.

After lunch Wanda walked out and opened the door of the tool shed. She couldn't believe the mess it was in. She shut the door immediately, then slowly opened it. "Where do I start," she spoke out loud. Just then George walked up to the door from the scrap yard. He and his boss, Wanda's' dad, had eaten a sack lunch in the scrap yard after a morning of wrecking car motors. It was a particular dirty greasy job.

"Hi, Wanda. Your dad asked me to come and get a pipe wrench. He said it is on the large workbench. This must be it," George said as he picked up the 15—inch pipe wrench. "Your dad says that you are going to clean this shed out so I can sleep in it—is that correct." Wanda still wasn't convinced that George was a safe person to become too friendly with like her mother was and like her mother wanted Wanda to become. But, she needed to at least show some measure of decency if she was going to be sincere in her accomplishing her Good Samaritan list toward this individual.

"Yes, but I don't know where to start. This is a mess." George saw Wanda's frustration in her face and wanted to ease it for her.

"Can I help you with this project?" he asked.

"Yes, you may," she answered. "However, you are busy working with the scrap iron."

"If you want, I will come here after supper this evening and help you."

"OK," Wanda answered, "but only for a half hour. I have a date with Bruce and won't be home until the movie is over. I will maybe have time to work on this project after the movie also."

"Is Bruce your boyfriend?" George asked Wanda knowing that he may be putting his nose where he shouldn't put it.

Chapter 2

"Yes he is," Wanda answered. It was a question that she was glad to answer for George. She needed to let him know that she had absolutely no interest in having any relationship with George.

Immediately after supper George and Wanda met in the tool shed and began to clean the place. George started with emptying the waste baskets and Wanda by sweeping the floor. George moved stuff around to make it easier for Wanda. Then, George moved around some of the benches and combined what was sitting atop of them to make room for the bed that Wanda's mother had designated for George to sleep on. By the time that was all done it was time for Wanda to leave for the movie with Bruce. Bruce walked through the tool shed door. "Wanda, your mom told me you were in this shed. Are you ready to go to the movie?"

"Yes I am," Wanda answered. She made no effort to introduce George to Bruce. George continued working on cleaning the tool shed. He worked on this project until 9:30. As he was leaving the shed, Wanda and Bruce were just returning from their movie date. Again, Wanda made no attempt to introduce George and Bruce to each other.

When Wanda walked into the kitchen, Mildred asked Wanda a question: "What did Bruce think about George?" Wanda said nothing. "You did introduce them to each other, didn't you?"

"No, I did not," Wanda answered as she was leaving to go to her room for the night. She turned around and said to her mother, "I cannot get excited about George. He is a tramp and dirty and he and

I have nothing in common. I do not like the business dad is in and that work is the only thing that George will ever be able to do."

Wanda was embarrassed when talking about George. She also thought that Bruce may think that George was someone who she was attracted to. That was the furthest thing from the truth and from her mind. At least that is what she wanted people and especially Bruce to think. It didn't take George long to grasp this feeling.

When George came into the kitchen he approached Mildred and said, "The tool shed is now ready to place the bed in there. One thing that I want to place somewhere in the shed is this picture of my family. I may never see them again, but I do not want to forget them." Mildred reached and took an 8 x 10 photo from George of his family.

"I will find a nice frame to put the picture in," Mildred said. She glanced at George and noticed tears starting to well up in his eyes. Wanda was also watching while drinking a glass of milk. She had no reaction.

At breakfast a few mornings later, a new subject was brought up by Wanda's father. After a week of staying in the home of Thomas and Mildred Olson, some people familiar with George's appearance were wondering what the status of his education was and more importantly what his army status was. Should he not be in the military? Some of the town did not have knowledge that his nationality was half Japanese. "George," Thomas said, "high school has already begun in Harriet. What grade should you be in?" George was very quiet for a short time. He then suddenly realized that he should not

Chapter 2

keep his host family in the dark about his background any longer, lest he lose his new happy home, no matter how temporary.

"My journey began a week before Mildred found me by the railroad track on your grass. In short—my parents and I agreed that I should run away from home." There was the whole range of doubt in the thoughts of those at the table: no way, I've heard of people doing that, that is really sad, and he's making this up.

The breakfast crowd was now waiting for him to go on with his story.

"The previous day, prior to my departure, I was refused acceptance into any of the United States military services because of my nationality. In addition to that, being I am half Japanese, I would need to go into an internment camp along with my family. I did not want to do that.

"My mother's heart almost broke that afternoon. She is probably still crying. After we went to church and ate a short picnic lunch by the train station, I quickly stepped on a boxcar ladder and disappeared from my family's sight." Mildred was shedding some tears, while Wanda just sat staring at the wall. George continued relating the escape story and the problems he had with the other passengers on the slow moving freight. George's host family sat listening to him while at the same time not knowing whether to believe him or not. He continued his story.

"I managed to get into an open boxcar. There were several other individuals in the same boxcar all being what most people would call bums, tramps, or hobos. A few of the men had just gotten paid from an onion farmer and one of them made the mistake of counting his pay in front of everyone in the boxcar. I found out that day it is something you do not do in a railroad boxcar in front of a group of bums.

Some big bruiser grabbed the man's billfold and pushed him out of the boxcar onto the westbound track. I was sure that he was injured from the sound he made when he hit the track. I quickly latched onto my backpack and jumped off the boxcar myself. When I found the poor guy he was out cold and lying on the track. I was sure that he had a broken leg and a head concussion.

"I managed to carry him to a house 500 feet from the track where a nice elderly lady offered a bed where he could rest. She called a doctor that lived nearby to come and treat him. I had a $10 bill on me and I left it with her to pay the doctor or hospital. Then I walked back to the railroad track and waited for another slow moving freight train. That is most of the story of my trip to your house."

Mildred, Wanda, and Thomas sat quietly for the next few seconds not knowing exactly how to react to George's story. "I have work to do in the scrapyard," he said as he stood up, "if you will all excuse me. Again, thank you for the very good breakfast, Mildred. One of these days I may even call you Mom."

"I wish you would," Mildred responded.

After the evening meal George helped Mildred carry and set up the bed in the tool shed for him to sleep on. The first night was not the most restful for George as the many trains made noises he'd never heard before. Having a single train pass by was bad enough. Once during the night two freight trains met, one going east and one going west. They each had 3 huge steam engines pulling them. The tool shed was only 30 feet from the tracks, being once a railroad repair section house. The vibration from the steel wheels clicking on the

Chapter 2

space between the rails was almost more than the human ear could withstand. George finally stuffed a piece of an old shirt in his ears. Only then could he get some sleep.

George was awake at 5 a.m. and decided to rise and began cutting apart some old machinery. A box of soda crackers and a can of Vienna sausages was all he needed to get him through the early morning hours. At about 7:30 Wanda and Mildred walked out of the house and got into the car. Apparently Wanda needed to be somewhere early. As the car drove past where George was working, George and Mildred waved at each other. Wanda looked straight ahead. He wondered what it would take for her to just act civil to him. Maybe, just patience and time.

As he torched up the scrap machinery that a customer had brought in the day before, George piled the pieces such that when he and Thomas loaded them onto the truck later, it could be done with ease. Because of the labor shortage in Harriet, the machinery to be scrapped was piling up much faster than the business could handle it.

George made the decision to start early every morning and work late at night. He took off on Saturdays at 4 pm and just relaxed. Sunday work was out of the question. On Sunday afternoon, Mildred and Wanda would make some cookies, or a batch of divinity fudge. It was a treat for everyone. That, and making popcorn became a Sunday afternoon family tradition.

August, 1942

On a morning in August, an announcement on the radio and an article in the Harriet Press newspaper told of the government's plan to begin a scrap collecting program to fill the shortage of raw materials in the United States. The program was called Collection of Materials for the War Effort. Many raw materials had been cut off because of the war, especially from the Far East. Thomas wondered how this program would affect his business of scrap metal. He also wondered how this program would be handled with the shortage of physical labor.

Slightly over a year earlier The Office of Civilian Defense had organized a salvage drive for rubber, tin, paper, and aluminum. The drives intensified when the United States entered the war. In the summer of 1942, the drive to secure even more tin was intensified. A Harriet Press reporter showed, with a drive-by of The Harriet dump ground, why so many more tin cans could be recovered. *"The tin in these rusty cans could never be recovered,"* the photo indicated. The article pointed out why these cans were so important to the war effort. Two tin cans contained enough tin for a syrette, which was used for administrating sedatives on the battlefield to prevent shock. Also, since tin was the only metal that wasn't harmed by salt water, it was used in shipping food overseas.

Every week the Harriet Press ran a report on what organization turned in the greatest weight of tin cans. There was competition in the schools, churches, 4H clubs, and even sewing groups.

Chapter 2

August 19

The morning paper printed an article that both Mildred and Thomas were afraid to face their friends and neighbors with. Thomas' entry into his favorite coffee shop that morning was also met with some cold shoulders. Jesse Sorenson and Fred Jacobson were the first ones to meet him at the door wanting to accuse their scrap metal friend of something. Jesse and Fred looked at Thomas with stares that said to him, "*What happened to this county's scrap iron?*" Finally Fred said it.

"So, Tommy, where is all of our scrap iron now? Coming back in the form of bullets in our dead boys? It also came back at Pearl Harbor, didn't it?" Immediately, a few of the other regular customers mildly expressed similar negative comments. Tommy had been expecting some of these comments to flare up in various parts of town. There was nothing he could do about it. When he had begun to sell to the Japanese only a few intelligence officials knew that the scrap iron was being used for weapons of war. Even as late as two weeks before the Pearl Harbor attack he heard a comment that none of the scrap iron coming from the Harriet, Wisconsin area was going to anyplace but agriculture machinery manufacturing in Japan. If the truth be known, Thomas had his doubts about this fact even at that time.

Thomas never said a word in response and took his coffee to a booth far from the normal café crowd. No one had the guts to join him. He wondered how long it would be before the entire town of Harriet found out that his hired boy was half Japanese. *How this will affect my scrap business is yet another worry on my mind.*

Thomas slowly walked out of the coffee shop and strolled along the Chicago and Northwestern Railroad tracks toward his home. As he got within the border of the scrap yard, George saw him walking and could see and realized that his boss was in a dreadful state of mind. George was cutting apart loads of horse driven farm machinery, preparing it for loading into a gondola car the next day. Thomas stopped and called out to George, "You are doing a good job in cutting up that machinery. I cannot believe that you learned to use an acetylene torch just a few weeks ago."

"I am doing the best I can. Maybe we can make enough profit so you can buy a power shear someday. Although they are dangerous to use, it would make our productivity increase. I read an article about it in your scrap metal trade magazine."

"George," Thomas said, "you and I need to talk. After supper, let's sit in the living room and put our heads together. I have many questions and you have a fresh mind."

At the dinner table, after the table prayer was said, Wanda spoke up. "George, I am supposed to ask you if you would like to talk to my high school counselor about continuing your high school education. He has been given some money to teach students who cannot meet the basic requirements for military service or have not graduated from high school." George sat quietly in his chair, eating his meal and sifting through his mind the proposal that Wanda had just presented to him. The question from Wanda was a little embarrassing and he wasn't ready for it.

"Can you give me a day or so to think about it? It's too big of a subject to swallow in one sitting."

"Take the entire weekend to think about it," Wanda responded.

Chapter 2

"One question I have: If I attend school where you go now, will any of the kids attack me or will they instead, protect me," George said jokingly.

"Don't worry," Wanda answered, "they are all good people."

George was beginning to become fond of Wanda. However, the feeling was not mutual. She had her own male interests with some of the boys in her class. George could only dream of a personal relationship with Wanda. He would be kind and considerate in his contact with her around the home and scrap business. In turn she tried to be kind to him and understood what he was attempting to do. He could only hope that someday she or some other female would take an interest in him. At this current time within the United States, the worst nationality one could be was one half Japanese. He made up his mind to remain at a social distance in his relationship with Wanda.

George also remembered his promise to Thomas—to be a behind the scenes body guard of Wanda's. *I think she should be able to protect herself—unless she meets up with some unsavory character*, he thought to himself.

Wanda did arrange for George to meet with the school counselor about continuing his education. He had quit school in the Los Angeles suburb where he lived. Unfortunately, it was the area where the greatest concentration of Japanese immigrants had settled. Trouble began when the Japanese bombed Pearl Harbor. Anti-Japanese public sentiments commenced the day after the bombing. Fights broke out between the American and Japanese students. Many of the Japanese families began to pull their children out of school. Within months many of the Japanese students were in the internment camps with their parents.

George was in the 10th grade when he dropped out of school in Los Angeles. Luckily he carried a copy of his school record with him when he hopped on the train in Los Angeles. Now in Herriot he needed to continue his work in the scrap yard, but was permitted to attend class after 6 pm two nights each week and on Sunday afternoon. He was warned by Mr. Fjeld that progressing at this speed may require another 2 years to obtain his high school diploma. He was told that he may be able to get credit for courses he took in California that the Harriet school did not offer. What George would really miss would be the social interaction with the other students, no matter what nationality they were. He was able to gain some of that social contact in the Youth Sunday school at church.

Wanda was told by George to not talk about him to the students and teachers where she was attending school, lest she make it difficult for her social association with them. "Also, Wanda, because of the anger caused by the shortage and rationing of food, it could easily spill over into fights and riots. You live your life, I will live mine, you and I can communicate at the dinner table, and things will be peaceful."

Chapter 2

One afternoon a nice lady from Olson's church came over to the Olson house. She came carrying a large plate covered with wax paper. She knocked at the Olson's kitchen door. Mildred walked over and opened the Kitchen screen door. "Doris, it is good to see you. Please come in."

"I have just made some cookies for your family and especially for your house guest," she said. "Wanda told me about him. I'll bet he has never tasted chocolate chip cookies."

"That is so kind of you, Doris," Mildred responded. "Let's you and I try out some along with some of the coffee that I just brewed."

When George came to the kitchen for his afternoon coffee break and tasted the cookies, he commented again, "I think I have died and gone to heaven."

CHAPTER 3

Fall of 1942

The news about the war in Europe and now in the Pacific was not very good. Mildred listened to the news every morning on the network radio stations and was able to keep up with the progress. Since her husband spent most of his time out where there was no radio to listen to, he left it up to her to inform him of any significant changes in the war's progress—good or bad.

It was December of 1942 when the weather turned cold in Harriet, Wisconsin. Both Thomas and George were working in the snow, cutting up scrap iron out of old farm machinery. No longer was the Olson scrap metal Company shipping the scrap to Japan. They were now selling the scrap iron to a company in Des Moines, Iowa. Because of the shortage of young men and even middle aged men, Thomas and George were doing all of the work themselves. It was bitterly cold at times. What made it extra cold was having to use thin gloves to operate the torch heads. Sheepskin mittens would have made it much warmer and comfortable, but more difficult to turn the knobs and pull the trigger.

Chapter 3

It took both men a longer time to dress in the mornings when the temperature was very cold. They needed at least one pair of long underwear, a pair of wool pants, a stocking cap with earmuffs, two pairs of wool socks, wool shirts, warm shoes and rubber boots to keep the feet dry. Because they needed to remain still when cutting with the torch, movement of their body to generate heat was not possible.

It was also important to keep their hands warm and dry. The best way was to wear a pair of gloves with an extra pair drying out by the warm stove. Some gloves were better than others in keeping the hands warm and dry.

During one of the weeks in the middle of January of 1943, it was below -10 degrees for the entire week. If it got much below that temperature, work would be found in the metals building sorting and cleaning non-ferrous metal.

When metal was sorted out, it needed to be all the same metal in the barrel or pail. If a bolt or another piece of metal was attached, it needed to be separated. Sometimes sharp chisels, wrenches, or the cutting torch, were needed to separate the different metals.

On February 15^h, 1943, an announcement was made by President Roosevelt asking the American public to begin collecting scrap materials to be used to make up for the shortage created from using certain materials for the war. This included all types of metal—steel, copper, aluminum, brass, cast Iron, and high tin metals. However, the shortage of items didn't stop with the metals. They also included scrap paper, old rags, grease and cooking fat, etc.

When Thomas came in for morning coffee, Mildred of course informed him of the announcement. "What would they want old rags and cooking fat for?" Mildred asked.

"Well," Thomas responded after taking a swig of hot coffee, "the cooking fat, along with scrap oil and grease, is used in the manufacture of explosives—I think. Maybe the old rags are used for the same purpose as I use them for—to clean hands, machinery, and maybe to clean the decks of ships. As far as other items that are in the category of surplus collectibles, I am not sure. Maybe the two wars has upset the shipping lanes of the countries from where certain products originated. I do know this—the work required in this announcement will give people all over America something meaningful to do."

Mildred and Wanda were cleaning the cupboards in the kitchen on a Saturday morning when Thomas came through the kitchen door. He was looking down and out like he had just lost his best friend. "What's wrong Tommy, you look very glum?" Mildred asked.

"I was just at the bank and they had bad news for me. They turned down my loan application." Mildred stopped what she was doing and looked at her husband.

"So what reason did they give?" she asked.

"What they told me and what the real reason was, are two different things. At least that is what I suspect."

"So what did they tell you?" Mildred inquired.

"Too risky, they said. But, the rumor going around is that my former association with the Japanese steel mills is the real reason. That is not all," Thomas continued, "the stores in town have shut off credit to me also. I don't know if we can keep George on with us."

"That is bad news," Mildred commented.

Chapter 3

"I will talk to George. I have yet to discuss with him what we are going to pay him. We do give him food and his sleeping quarters. How much more we need to give him is up in the air."

"I hope we do not lose him," Wanda said in a surprising comment. Thomas and Mildred looked at Wanda, wondering why her change of heart. "I just don't care about me needing to work in the scrap yard. That's all."

Thomas was reading the Harriet Press one evening and saw an article where pilots in the U.S. and Great Britain were in need of sheepskin vests and helmets. The problem was that to get these skins to tan, the sheep would need to either be butchered or die of natural causes. The sheep or large lambs would then have to be skinned and sent to the tanning firm and fur manufacturer. "Hey George, come here once," Thomas said to his only employee.

"Yes, Mr. Olson, I'm here. What can I do for you?" George responded.

"Have you ever skinned a sheep or lamb?" Thomas asked.

"No, I have not. I've eaten a couple meals of both mutton and lamb, but I didn't care for either. Why do you ask?"

"I think we should venture into the sheepskin business. Pilots in Great Britain, New Zealand, Canada, and of course The United States, need sheepskin vests and helmets. Thousands of pilots are being trained in both the U.S. and Britain. The paper here says there is a shortage of sheepskin vests. Much of the world's supply comes from the Pacific Rim nations. We have many sheep farmers around Harriet."

George blurted in, "I have seen some of them dead and rotting in pastures and barnyards when I am cutting up machinery on these sheep ranches. In fact, when I was at the Perkins Ranch just this morning Fred was telling me that he lost 10 sheep last night—the neighbor's dogs killed them. I saw that their skins were not torn up. The dogs were not hungry for mutton, they were just hungry to kill sheep."

"Come," Mr. Olson said, "let's jump in the car and drive out there and ask Mr. Perkins if we can buy the skins off the dead sheep. We will need to stop at the hardware store and get a couple of knives."

"Also a knife sharpener," George added.

Thomas and George drove 10 miles north of Harriet to a large sheep ranch. The wife of the owner gave them permission to remove the skins from the dead sheep. The sheep were still slightly warm and some of the ewes had about-to-be-born lambs inside of them. This situation added to the rancher's loss.

In two hours the two of them were back at the scrap yard with 10 skins from Mr. Perkin's dead sheep. "Mrs. Perkins was well satisfied with a price of 50 cents apiece for the skins," Thomas commented.

"How about if we shear the wool off of the pelts and make some extra money?" George suggested.

"That sounds like a great idea," Thomas said. "Maybe, if we offer to pay the sheep ranchers something for their dried sheep skins, they will skin the dead sheep and bring them to us. I have a sheep shearing kit in the house."

Thomas began thinking of what other pieces of fur could be used for pilot vests. There were raccoon, badger, wolf, wolverine, beaver, opossum, and skunk—all long haired wild animals. "They will make warm vests for pilots," Mr. Olson said. "The supply of this fur comes from the United States as well as far Eastern Asian and European

Chapter 3

countries. Because of the tens of thousands of pilots being trained and deployed, the demand will become enormous. Although these are long-haired wild fur, the fur manufacture will shear the long guard hairs off so the fur will be smooth and silky. The guard hairs are long and stiff."

Thomas and George decided to take on this task as a winter time enterprise. Because of the demand due to the war, the price for these fur bearing animals increased in price. The fur on badger was probably the best for pilot vests. Thomas found another market for this fur. In Europe and the U.S., they used badger fur to make shaving brushes.

Thomas found a clothing manufacture in Brooklyn that was interested in making pilot vests and fur lined helmets from the fur. The Olson Scrap Iron and metal Company would supply the raw fur from animals around the Harriet area. The Brooklyn Company contacted other fur buyers around the country and made connections with them. A building on the Olson property needed to be built for processing the animals, along with a freezer to preserve them and to keep them from spoiling.

The next challenge was to obtain an abundant labor supply. There were no young men available, as the war had gobbled up this labor supply. George suggested that they hire some of the strong women in Harriet to process the animals. This was an easy task as many woman in town wished to make money. Even mothers with young children would apply if they could find other women who would babysit for them while they worked. Mildred organized some of the churches to perform this task, whereby the churches would use the babysitting money for their mission work.

In addition to the profit made from the fur, the fat scraped off of the skins was a source of raw material used to make glycerin for gunpowder by the government. The Olson Fur Company collected 30 gallon barrels of this commodity in the first week of the fur season and sold them to a dealer in Duluth. The animal carcasses were ground up for fur farm feed and fertilizer. George found a source for heating the wood stoves inside of their own buildings. He would make a baseball size ball out of the raccoon fat, freeze the ball, and throw it into the wood stove. Care needed to be taken so that the outside of the stove didn't get cherry red hot. The animal fat was very flammable.

Later one afternoon the noise of a car in the driveway got Mildred's attention. At the same time she looked out the kitchen window and saw a government car parked in the driveway. Her heart suddenly sank. *What does he want?* She asked herself. Then she thought of their acquired son George. *They have come to get him,* she said to herself with a certain amount of fear. She walked to the front door, opened it, and walked toward the man in a black suit standing by his car.

"Good afternoon Ma'am," he said in a businesslike tone, "is your husband Thomas home?" Mildred immediately wondered how this man knew her husband's name.

"I see that he is coming up the road for his afternoon coffee," Mildred answered, still slightly shaking. Thomas saw the government car and got a slight scare like Mildred had.

"Mr. Olson," the tall man said, "my name is Felix Wilcox. I am from the county seat office and would like to talk to you." The two men shook hands and Thomas led him into the house.

Chapter 3

"Let's sit at the kitchen table," Thomas replied. "How can I help you?"

George, without the Olson's knowing, had slipped into the bathroom to get a bar of soap for the bathroom sink in the tool shed sleeping quarters where he was living. He happened to be there as the session with the government official began. He stood in the bathroom as the conversation continued. He also suspected that the government official may be after his hide and was going to send him back to California. George was ready to run to the nearby woods and hide.

"I'm sure that you have heard the news," Mr. Wilcox began, "that the President is asking for the people of the country to start collecting materials to aid in the shortage of certain raw materials. Many of these materials are needed in the war effort. Being you are in the scrap metal business, we think you would be a logical candidate to be the chairman of this county's scrap collection effort." Both Thomas and Mildred listened intently as the gentleman talked for the next 5 minutes. Then, he stopped while waiting for either of the Olson's to respond.

Thomas finally asked, "give us some more details on the job—the pay, the involvement of the government, restrictions, the ability to keep our scrap business going, and any help from the feds." At that point Mr. Wilcox opened his notebook and put on his glasses.

"First of all, the pay will be $100.00 per week. Next, you will be under my supervision, although you may not see me for weeks at a time. I will have several counties under my direction. Also, because your business is scrap metal, we expect that you will desire to keep it going. You really will act independently of me."

"Good," Thomas responded, "I was hoping you would say that."

"But, there is a catch," Felix alerted.

"Oh-oh," Mildred broke in, "here comes the bad news."

"Not really," the government official countered. "The catch is that you will need to be hiring your own labor and paying them. And, as you may be aware, almost all of the potentially good workers are in the military, or about to go into the military service."

"That <u>will</u> be a problem—yes it will," Thomas agreed. He also had on his mind the problem of his business employing a young boy who was admittedly half Japanese.

"Another important item," the official continued, "and this is the reason we choose to come and see you instead of some fly-by-night individual. The government will be collecting all types of materials from the public. Much of the stuff will be collected and donated by The Boy Scouts, churches, social clubs, grade school classes, women's clubs, and dozens of other groups. All of this stuff, and I do mean stuff, will need to be kept separate from the metal and other items that you pay for to your customers. Most of the items will be donated and some you will pay customers for. This could be an accounting nightmare. You will need to be as honest as a 'George Washington'."

"You won't find a more honest scrap metal dealer in all the state than my husband, Thomas," Mildred reassured Mr. Wilcox.

"We know that for a fact, ma'am. We have known this for weeks."

"How do you know that?" Thomas asked with a surprised look. Mr. Wilcox closed his notebook and smiled.

"Mr. Olson, do you remember 3 days ago, when two people came in each with a pail of burned #1 copper wire? And then, just yesterday, a lady came in with a trailer load of scrap iron?"

"Yes I do," Thomas replied. "The lady had a little puppy dog named Molly. I fed Molly a piece of a hot dog I had in the ice box."

Chapter 3

"In each of these customers, you were watched very closely. You made sure that the scale beam balanced, even though the customer wasn't watching you or the scale, and you wrote the amount correctly on the ticket. When you paid her, you made it clear on the paper the correct multiplication. It was a completely honest transaction."

"I do that with every customer," Thomas agreed. Then the Government Official added:

"Many scrap dealers follow this same procedure," the government official said, "except for the part where they write down the weight amount. The scale will balance but the dishonest dealers write down a lesser amount than the actual weight. If the customer notices it and says something, the dishonest scrap dealer will say, 'whoops, I made a mistake.' You are a very honest businessman, Mr. Olson and you would not do that," the government official concluded. "That is why we need you to chair the 'County Scrap Drive.'"

Suddenly, George, still standing in the bathroom, knew he had a golden opportunity to help his employer make a decision, while at the same time possibly solving his own predicament. He quickly walked into the kitchen. "Would you permit me to enter this conversation?" George spoke out boldly knowing he was risking his job, Mr. Olson's potential livelihood, and his current happy home. Mildred quickly spoke up.

"George, please speak up," she said.

"My name is George Robinson. If you haven't guessed by now, I am half Japanese. I am also a fulltime employee of Mr. Olson. All of the United States military services rejected me from volunteering because of my nationality. I believe that I can be a big asset to Mr. Olson's scrap business if I can stay with him." George stopped at that point and just looked at the official, waiting for a reaction. Both

Mildred and Thomas were wondering where George's comments were going next.

"You sound like a good employee," Mr. Wilcox remarked.

"There is only one problem," George continued. "The government is placing the west coast Japanese into camps, including my family. If the military comes and gets me, Mr. Olson will lose his most valuable employee—at this point his only employee. So let me propose a solution to this whole situation. You guarantee that the United States government won't come and get me to throw me into an internment camp and Mr. Olson will agree to be this county's scrap drive chairman. This business has been, is now, and will be until the end of the war, a great asset to the collection of scrap iron and metal."

"You've got it!" the government official enthusiastically announced as he stood up to leave. "I will make sure our military police do not touch you. I will be back tomorrow morning to discuss the collection procedure of the various material items. By the way, how in the world did you get to Harriet, Wisconsin from California?"

"I hopped a freight," George unashamedly announced."

"You seem happy about it. So you can now sing the song, 'Hallelujah, I'm a Bum.'"

"That is correct," George agreed.

After the Federal official drove away, Mildred asked George, "what's this 'Hallelujah, I'm a Bum' business."

"It's a song from a 1933 American musical comedy, <u>Hallelujah! I'm A Bum</u>. It was made popular in 1926 by singer Al Jolson. It was written by Harry McClintock. Let me sing some of it for you."

Hallelujah! I'm a bum, Hallelujah bum again
Hallelujah! Give us a handout and revive us again

I went to a house and I knocked on the door
A lady says, "Bum, bum, you been here before"

I went to a house, and I asked for some bread
a lady says, "Bum, bum, the baker is dead"

Oh why don't you work like other folks do
how in the world can I work when there's no work to do?

Oh why don't you work like other folks do
How can I get a job when you're holding down two

Oh, I love my boss and my boss loves me
and that is the reason I'm so hungry

Oh why don't you save all the money you earn
well if I didn't eat, I'd have money to burn

Oh, I like my boss, he's a good friend of mine
and that's why I'm starving out in the breadline

Whenever I get all the money I earn
the boss will be broke and to work he must turn

Final chorus:

Hallelujah! I'm a bum, Hallelujah bum again
Hallelujah! Lord, give us a handout, we thank you, Amen.

"If you don't mind George, I will call you that," Thomas said.

"I really don't mind," George said. "If I never became a bum and rode the train out to Harriet, I would probably be in the internment camp right now and wouldn't be with you nice people."

"Well, I don't think that the song and name is very kind to George," Wanda said as she had just walked into the house and heard the end of the song.

Early next morning Thomas and George met for a scrap salvage meeting at Ginny's café. Both of them agreed that it was ok for them to be seen together in public. The town of Harriet's gossip mill had chewed up the tale of George arriving on the Chicago and Northwestern freight in July of 1942. There was nothing more to spit out. Thomas began the meeting after they had ordered breakfast.

"We need to discuss how we are going to handle the collection of scrap from not only the town of Harriet, but from the surrounding farms and small towns. We need to accomplish this task such that we make a profit and in an honest and above board manner, and at the same time give pride to the groups collecting the surplus. Many of the items collected will be paid according to their weight—Items like steel, copper, aluminum, etc. All other items collected will have no money transferred: like newspaper, clothes, old phonograph records, etc. and will need only a thank you or some kind of reward or recognition."

Chapter 3

"I think that our biggest challenge will be in finding places to store the stuff. Also, the people collecting will be wanting something in return for their work," George responded. "Maybe a big 'thank you' would be enough. Or, just making them feel good that they have contributed to the war effort."

"Maybe a certificate with their name on it and a photo of a soldier carrying a gun," Thomas added. "I will find out if some recognition item is available from the state or county."

It was Wanda's senior year at Harriet High School. She was working hard to hopefully become one of the honor students in her class. She was having difficulty, however, with math. She mentioned it to her parents at supper on a Friday evening. "How is school going, Wanda?" Mildred asked.

"Most of it is OK, except for math," she replied. "I could use some help. I have a big test on Monday and I am not ready for it." It was then that George interrupted the conversation.

"Why don't I help Wanda with her math, if she will let me?" The family just looked at George, not expecting him to be of any help, let alone to offer any. The family weren't real sure how George was at math. In fact they weren't sure how he was at school in general.

Wanda wasn't too sure about George helping her. Her mind was pretty much made up that she wasn't wanting to get involved with George in any manner. Her folks sat at the table waiting for Wanda to respond. "Ok, let me get my book and see if you can help me," Wanda said without showing much excitement.

"Are the Japanese good at math?" Mildred asked. George was quick to answer.

"We Japanese, even we who are only half Japanese, fully believe that in 10 to 20 years Japan will dominate the industrialized world in math and many other sciences. It would be sooner if the Japanese government wouldn't have attacked the United States at Pearl Harbor. Then more of our kids could attend college in the U.S. speaking English."

That night George sat at the table with Wanda and helped her with her algebra until 11 p.m. It was the first time he had spent any length of time with her. He was very patient teaching her. Her mom and dad watched and listened the entire time while reading various periodicals. When they were finished Wanda felt confident that she would pass her test on Monday. "Let me know how you make out with your test, Wanda," George said.

The next morning Thomas was visited by a farmer north of Harriet. He had 4 big steam engine tractors to sell for scrap. They weighed 12 tons each, were considered antiques and no longer usable even for spare parts. They were old, some of their parts were wearing out, and the owner was about to retire with no children to take over the farm. He tried to find some interested young man who would be willing to take over the farming operation with the option to buy. However, with many of possible candidates having gone off to war and not being assured of when or if they would be returning, the owner decided to sell the steam engines for scrap. The 4 engines were bought by Thomas with a check written out by Mildred.

Chapter 3

Now there was the problem of how to wreck the steam engines and get the flywheels and housings around the engine in small enough pieces to ship and to fit into the factory and foundry hoppers. The answer was to purchase dynamite to blow the thick cast iron parts into smaller pieces. A special permit was needed from the city of Harriet to use dynamite. And, of course, safety was of the upmost importance. When the dynamite was used, the Harriet neighbors near the scrap yard were warned beforehand so that they weren't scared out of their wits.

After several months Thomas finally had time to sit down with George and discuss his compensation for working in the scrap yard. "George, I am sorry that I have not visited with you before now about how much I will pay you for working in our business. I have been so busy, rather, we have been so busy."

"No problem, Mr. Olson," George responded. "You have a mountain of worries on your mind. I have viewed this matter as not what you can pay me, rather, _if_ you can pay me. I feel that you feeding me, giving me a place to live, providing me with clothes, shoes, and other essentials is all the compensation I need. That includes any tape, salve, etc. that I need when I burn myself with hot torch sparks."

"Well George, I'm glad you feel that way. But I am going to place in writing a contract that will give you a gradual partial ownership of the Olson Scrap Metal Company after you have been here for 5 years. The amount will not be great, but since I have no heir to leave the business to when I pass on, I will leave part of it to you. Wanda has no interest in the business. Plus the fact that I can trust you, and you are like the son that we lost in the late 1930s.

"Meanwhile, I will continue to pay you $1.00 per hour. That is the amount I have been paying you since September 1. That is about 60 days after the day you arrived on our lawn. We will meet about this matter once a month at which time we will review your progress. The war should be over in 5 years. How does that sound?"

"Sounds good," George answered in an appreciative tone. "But, honestly, you could pay me nothing and I would be satisfied. Also, your business and place of residence has protected me from being interned in the camps in California." George had something he wished to ask his boss.

"I notice that there are piles of rubbish in the field that exists on various sections of your property. What are they from?" George's boss broke out with a wide smile and laugh.

"You discovered them," Thomas responded.

"Discovered what?" George asked.

"Those piles have been sitting there since the time I began this scrap iron business years ago. The first two years when I would sell non-ferrous metal to a scrap dealer in Duluth, Minnesota, I needed to clean up the mess left in my metals building each time I sold a truckload. The last step in that cleaning process was to sweep the floor and dump all of the dust and little pieces of metal into a wheel barrow and haul it to the back 40. I thought that someday I would have dirt hauled in and completely cover the piles. Why do you ask, George?"

"If you wanted to compensate me for working for you, Mr. Olson, in some extra way, you could let me have those piles. I could dig them up, sort out the metal, and sell them back to you at the going price on that day."

Chapter 3

"George, we have a deal—the piles are all yours. Plus $1.00 per hour for your regular work. By the way George, you may call me Thomas—I don't mind."

"Well, Mr. Olson, I may call you Thomas every once in a while. But out of respect for my elders and what I have been taught, I prefer to call you Mr. Olson, especially in front of other people."

The next week George started working after the evening meal on the piles of floor sweepings dumped on the open field behind the scrap yard. He was finding mostly small pieces of non-ferrous metal that were of little weight. However, he noticed that as he placed them in gallon coffee cans, the weight was beginning to add up. He was also learning all of the various metals of value. There was #1 copper wire, # 2 copper wire, light brass, yellow brass, red brass, aluminum, lead, zinc, pewter, block tin, and of course steel. Most of the tin and steel had rusted greatly while in the ground for years. As he had a coffee can filled with a particular metal he would bring it to Thomas, would have him weigh it, and get paid with a check written and signed by Mildred.

"You should weigh each metal and write the amount on a piece of paper and then give the paper to Mildred or me," Thomas commented, "I trust your judgment in weighing."

"That may be true," George responded, "but this way it will keep me honest. My dad always taught me to 'Flee from All Appearance of Evil.'"

Two days later George was cutting-up farm machinery when he experienced a new kind of pain. A fairly large piece of molten metal fell on his shoe when he was cutting steel with the cutting torch. Somehow the piece of metal worked its way between his shoe tongue and his sock. Because his sock took a few seconds to burn through, the pain never started until it reached the bare foot. By the time George had managed to take off his shoe, the molten metal had burned a good size spot in his foot, through the skin, and into the flesh. The smell of burnt flesh coupled with smoldering sock material and burnt shoe tongue leather was very strong and somewhat sickening.

George took off his shoe and hobbled up to the house. He sat down on a chair on the porch and exposed the top of his foot to the warm summer air. "Mildred, could you please come and help me with something?" He voiced loud enough so she would hear him. Mildred came right away.

"Oh, what happened to you, George?"

"I guess I burned myself."

"This is a job for a nurse. Wanda!" Mildred yelled out.

"Yes, Mom, What can I do for you?" Wanda responded, expecting a simple task from her mother.

"You can do something for George," Mildred answered. "At the same time you can practice being a nurse. Look at the top of his foot." Not only was George's foot burned, it was bleeding. The red hot metal had burned deep into the flesh on top of his foot. Wanda made a grimace and turned her face in the opposite direction, indicating she had no desire to treat his foot. Mildred brought a basin of clean water, a bar of homemade soap, some Raleigh's Carbolic Salve, two pieces of gauze, and a roll of adhesive tape.

Chapter 3

Wanda sat on the sofa looking toward George, face covered with her hands, and once again showing her displeasure of having to help George. Mildred could see this in Wanda's facial expression. "Well, Wanda, are you going to help George, or do I do it?"

Finally, Mildred did the doctoring on George, while Wanda sat still and just observed. Soon he hobbled outside toward the scrap pile and continued his work.

George never came in for dinner that noon. Why? Mildred and Wanda did not know. Later, Thomas gave his opinion. "I think Wanda still has some hang-up about George that I can't explain and I wonder if she can explain. There is some problem between George and Wanda."

Two days later George asked Mildred if she could look at his burn to see if it was healing properly. Wanda, who was just coming down from the upstairs interrupted and said, "Let me look at it." Everyone was quiet.

"Please do," George quickly responded. She came down the stairs, sat down on the sofa next to the patient, and began to take off his shoe, sock, and bandage. As she looked at the wound, her face once again turned to a grimace.

"George," she sounded out with a sense of concern, "your foot is infected. You need to see a doctor. Mother, we need to take George to see Dr. Thysell. George has an infection on his foot." Wanda quickly wrapped up his foot and helped him to the car. They were soon at the doctor's office where he received a shot of antibiotic to prevent the spread of the infection. On the way home George asked Wanda why she wouldn't treat the burn right after it first happened.

"I don't know why. For some unknown reason, I did not want to. That is bad, since I am planning to be a nurse someday."

"That is bad," George replied in a semi scolding voice. "What are you going to do if the U.S. Army calls you to be a nurse and a soldier is wounded on the battle field? Or, if you are asked to treat one of my Japanese brothers? Will you treat them?"

Wanda had no answer. George began to see the problem Wanda was having, but he did not know how to fix it, or how to help Wanda fix it.

Once a week George would walk to the State Bank of Harriet where he would deposit his weekly check. He would occasionally stop at Emily's flower shop and pick up a single rose for either Wanda or Mildred. Sometimes Emily would let him pick through the "throw-away" flower bin to make up a bouquet each for Mildred and Wanda. He would buy a nice glass vase to place them in.

Some nights he would have Mildred or Wanda walk out to where he was working, with his supper. He did this for two reasons—it gave the Olson family a chance to talk freely about topics that did not pertain to him. Also, he wouldn't need to clean up twice after his regular work stopped at about 5 pm.

One evening when Wanda brought George's meal out to him, she brought Bruce with her. George and Bruce had never been formally introduced. "Hi Bruce," George said to him. "Thanks for bringing me something to eat." Wanda immediately felt rather foolish for not having introduced them before.

"Hi George," Bruce responded. "Do you ever miss your friends back on the west coast?" George wondered why this question. Maybe

Chapter 3

Bruce wanted to make conversation with him and he couldn't think of any other thing to say.

"Yes I do miss them. I was on a soccer team that I had to leave. They were all Japanese except 3 players. We had a winning team. I had a girlfriend that I liked, but was glad when I left since it solved a big problem." Wanda became inquisitive and asked him about it.

"What problem did it solve George?" George stopped digging and sorting metal and just looked at the ground.

"She was Buddhist." Nothing else was further said. Both Wanda and Bruce were quiet for about 30 seconds. Finally, Wanda asked the obvious question.

"What happened? Did she not want you?"

"No," George responded. "She was not accepted by my parents and her parents did not accept me. I was Christian and she was Buddhist. We were not the same in our beliefs. A relationship like that would never work." George made that statement especially for Wanda and Bruce. He knew from talking to her parents that Bruce was not a Christian and Wanda was. The Thomas's were not in opposition to their daughter going with Bruce, only that there were other boys in their church's youth group who were Christians. That was enough discussion on that topic, George thought, and he decided to move it to another topic.

"How is school going for you two?" George asked.

"12th grade is not as easy as I thought it would be," Wanda answered. "But, it is a good warm up for my entry into college."

"How about you, Bruce," George asked. Bruce took a little more time to answer.

"It's also a little hard for me," Bruce responded. "Maybe I will go right into the army right after I graduate." All three were silent for the next couple of minutes. Finally, both Wanda and Bruce stood up and were preparing to walk back to the house.

"Thanks for bringing supper to me," George said. "I will see you another time."

George had not been in contact with his family on the west coast since he left there for Harriet in July, 1942. He asked Mildred to have Mr. Wilcox contact him or have him stop sometime. Maybe he could find out where his family was located.

Two days later, Mr. Wilcox stopped by just as the family was eating dinner. "Is 'Hallelujah I'm a Bum' in," Mr. Wilcox asked?

"I'm here," George answered with a smile of approval.

"How can I help you?" he asked. What George was about to ask Mr. Wilcox was somewhat private, but not to his Harriet family.

"I need to find out where my Japanese family is located on the west coast."

"I have already done that," Mr. Wilcox replied. "They are in Stockton, California. I was careful not to let on that I was searching the information for their son. So you won't have to worry." Mrs. Olson set an extra plate for the government official.

They had a cordial discussion on a variety of topics related to the wars and the collection of scarce war materials. The collection and storage of the materials that the Olson Scrap Metal Company was using was being recorded and copied by many other small towns around Harriet.

Chapter 3

George needed to somehow make contact with his family without leaving a paper trail back to Harriet for the authorities to come and get him. Even the use of phone contact would be very risky since the FBI and other information gathering agencies would be plugged into every internment camp on the west coast. He needed to think of a way to make contact in a unique manner.

George knew the maiden name of his mother and the name and address of the camp where his family was living. The first step was to write a birthday card to his mother at the internment camp. It wasn't his mother's birthday any time soon, but that didn't make any difference. His birthday card greeting read:

"*Dear Missionary Bernice: Just to let you know that I arrived in Dale, Minnesota in fine shape. I miss the family and all of the animals. The gingerbread cookies were delicious. Love, Joseph.*"

The next step was to address the card to Bernice Robinson. 1717 North Main Street, Stockton, California. Then, place the birthday card in a plain envelope, address it to Postmaster, Box 224, Miami, Florida.

Along with the birthday card, George placed a note for the postmaster which read: Postmaster: Please mail this card from your post office.

CHAPTER 4

According to the owners of the Olson Scrap Metal business, Thomas and Mildred Olson and their only employee George Robinson, the government scrap collection program seemed to be questionable in the direction it was going. Many of the items collected could never be used to remake usable products for the war effort. The program did, however, motivate the public into getting behind the war effort in a way people could feel good about themselves. They felt that they were doing their part for the war effort by collecting various items that were otherwise being dumped into landfills or burned up. Items such as metal cans which had a high tin metal content used in certain military parts were even collected and used. Otherwise these cans would go into landfills.

Many of the items collected were not economically feasible in converting to what was intended. The public were viewing any item laying around as something that could be converted into a material for use in the war effort. The owners of the scrap metal businesses all over the nation were wondering where they would store all of these items, where they would ship them, who would pay for the shipping, where would they dump them if no industry or governmental agency wanted them.

Chapter 4

The next morning the government official, Mr. Wilcox, drove up with his car and grabbed some notebooks with writing on each of them. The notebooks contained loose-leaf pages gathered together under various headings. George and Mr. Olson invited Mr. Wilcox into the kitchen. Mildred had coffee all made and ready in the pots. Mr. Wilcox began the meeting. "First of all, I need to tell you that in addition to the various collection drives throughout the United States, the government will soon start rationing several items. Two of them will be coffee and sugar."

"That is not good news for all of the Scandinavian folk in this community," Mr. Olson commented. "What else is the government wanting us to ration?" The official opened up his notebook to the list.

"The reason items are being rationed is because the supply routes have been cut off by the Japanese on the high seas," Mr. Wilcox said. At that point George broke into the conversation.

"Let me inform all of you that I consider myself an American citizen, not a Japanese citizen. So you can say anything you wish about that country and not hurt my feelings. I think that the Japanese were out of their skulls to bomb Pearl."

"Thank you for that comment, Mr. Robinson," Mr. Wilcox said, "I am glad you made that clear. By the way, do you know why the United States is interning Japanese on the west coast? I was informed this just last night."

"I have been wondering that ever since I heard on the news that they were doing that," George said. "Why would they do that to us seemingly good people?" Mr. Wilcox lifted up his coffee cup indicating his desire for an additional cup. Mildred reached over to the stove and grasped the coffee pot and poured another cup for all those present at the table.

"Here is the reason that Americans don't know. Prior to the bombing of Pearl Harbor, some of the Japanese who were living in Honolulu and other locations on the Hawaiian Islands, became undercover agents for the Japanese Navy, and took photos of our naval ships and armaments. Some of the agents would hire pilots of small planes and have them fly over the ships in the harbor and snap photos of them. That is the reason the Pearl Harbor bombing was so successful. Think of what other undercover Japanese agents could do if asked, by doing the same thing on the west coast of United States."

"You are correct," George answered. "I don't think our country has any other choice but to intern the Japanese. I wouldn't doubt if the Japanese are planning right now to attack some of the ports on our west coast in the near future. Just think of what damage Japanese kamikaze pilots could do to Los Angeles, Seattle, San Diego, and other cities."

"They are starting to ration gas in some places in the US, but not for the reason you think," Mr. Wilcox said. "You see, we have an abundant amount of gas and oil within our borders but not with rubber for the Tires. Officials think that if people are limited in their driving because of a supposed gas shortage, then we will cut down on our driving and save on rubber and tires also. They are probably correct."

"I have a question for you Mr. Wilcox," Thomas said.

"Ask it Mr. Olson," the government official answered.

"How long do you think that the war is going to last?"

"Remember now, Mr. Olson," Mr. Wilcox replied, "we are talking about two wars involving 3 major countries, a multitude of small

Chapter 4

countries, and virtually every nationality on earth. First of all the U. S. was surprised by the attack by the Japanese. We never saw it coming, although, I have heard that some of our people in Washington were aware that an attack was imminent. I also think that only our most learned and skilled Generals knew that we would be fighting on two fronts at one time. It has really drained our manpower resources so that persons like yourself have a hard time finding men to work.

"One other point, it appears now that the United States military complex is gearing up to a point where the Japanese military has awakened a sleeping giant, like one of their Japanese generals commented. I believe that because of our superior industrial potential and will to fight and win, the war will not be long. But then again we have two wars to win. Maybe our scientists will come up with a new type of weapon to hasten the war's end."

"Let's hope so," Mr. Olson added.

The meeting lasted for another hour and many additional cups of coffee.

Wanda graduated from Harriet high school in May, 1943 and decided to enroll right away in a college about 80 miles from Harriet. Her reason was to get out of the small town of Harriet. Most of her classmates felt the same.

She decided to enroll in a pre-nursing program in June of 1943. Although she was initially happy to get away from the small community of Harriet, she missed her family. While her relationship with George started out in the summer of 1942 less than accepting, she had gradually become more tolerant of his presence around the home and scrap yard. She knew that he had an itch for her and could always tell when he was watching her. However, he never made a pass at her, never asked her on a date, never spoke to her in a sensual manner, and was always ready to help her with anything he could. He always treated her in a respectful manner. The reverse from Wanda to George was mostly the opposite. He kept thinking that his time would come, if he was just patient.

Wanda became friends with many of the boys she met at college. She had a part time job at a hospital and even dated a couple of the student doctors at a nearby hospital. George did on two occasions write to Wanda with news of what was happening on the home front. She never answered his letters.

In the first year after George's arrival on the Olson green lawn, Thomas' business progressed faster than either Thomas or Mildred had ever expected. The need for new U.S. Military equipment and the scrap that was needed to produce them had replaced the pre-war steel contracts that the firm shipped to Japan, by several times. The County Scrap Surplus Chairman's salary added to Mr. Olson's financial increase and profitability. Both Thomas and George were constantly finding new ways to make a profit on some aspect of their scrap and surplus enterprise.

The collection of scrap materials became more and more of a challenge to the business. Individuals and organizations were

Chapter 4

collecting items that could be classified more as trash and junk, than as scarce strategic materials. Thomas finally asked George one afternoon, "What are we going to do with all of these piles of stuff, and I do mean stuff?"

"I have an idea," George responded. "I see that someone has an old building on the other side of town that they wish to get rid of. How about if we move it over here and build some 4ft x 4ft x 4ft wooden boxes to throw the collected surplus items in—a box for each item."

Both Thomas and George drove over to the other side of town and were able to negotiate a deal with the business that had the building they wished to get rid of. They would move the building to the Olson Scrap Yard in trade for some scrap 3-inch pipe that the Olsons had for sale. Within one week the building was moved, along with two piles of good 2 inch wood and some scrap plywood. This wood was used to build the wooden boxes to store the many salvage items that the people in the town and county were bringing in.

Some farmer had brought in a trailer load of gallon paint cans filled with various colors of paint. Thomas suggested that the girls, Mildred and Wanda, spend any spare time painting the inside and outside of the boxes. This would prevent the wood from decaying due to moisture.

The main salvage item that was stored in these boxes was scrap paper. The paper could not get wet or it would grow moldy and become useless. Mildred took charge of filling the boxes with paper as it came in. Any paper that people brought in wet would need to be dumped in back of the building. It would eventually rot into the ground.

Mildred stacked the newspaper in cardboard boxes that were not too big and could be lifted fairly easy—not over 50 pounds and could be easily stacked. It didn't take long for a 4 ft. x 4 ft. x 4 ft. wooden box to be filled.

Freight boxcars were brought in and loaded with paper and shipped to one of three locations where they were processed into various products. The business would make a fairly good profit for their work.

George happen to notice that many of the people were bringing in old magazines, some that were 20 and 30 years old. After supper, he would go into the old shed and look for old Look, Life, Saturday Evening Post, and other popular magazines. He brought them back to his sleeping quarters. He had the idea that when the war was over these periodicals would be in demand, especially by the military men and women coming back from the two fighting fronts. Certain newspapers would also be in demand. As these men and women were gone during this period, there would be a market to them also.

There were many hobos, bums, and tramps that continued to frequent the Chicago and Northwestern Railroad Tracks. Most of these individuals were always looking for a handout of food. Mildred was a ready and willing contributor, being that she was a good Christian. She would always have a plate of meat sandwiches all made up in the refrigerator to hand out. She would place a couple of them in a bag along with two cookies and a large pickle. She would also place in the bag a gospel of John. Mildred knew that the men and women did not live by bread alone—they also needed the gospel.

Wanda did not approve of this Christian practice. She thought that many of these men and women were taking advantage of her mother's generosity. She also thought that these men should work

Chapter 4

for the food. Sometimes a few extra men were needed to help load a carload of scrap. The Olson Scrap and Metal Company would hire these men from along the railroad track. As soon as the work was completed the men would be paid in cash. Mildred would feed them 3 meals that day. Unfortunately, quite often the cash Mildred placed in their hands would go directly to the Harriet bars.

George was surprised and somewhat overjoyed one noon when Mildred informed him that he had received a letter from someone in Miami, Florida. It was from his father in the internment camp. The letter was addressed to *Hallelujah I'm a Bum*. The letter read: "I am glad you are well. We are well and happy. The people here are treating our people well—from God's Servant." The letter was sent from the Postmaster in Miami, Florida.

"Well, I guess that answers my questions about the status of my family," George said with excitement. "Somehow I will need to go see them, sometime. But not until this war is over."

"Maybe you can ride a bus or take a train the next time you make the trip," Mildred commented. "Or, you could hop a freight again."

Thomas and George were getting calls in their scrap business for salvageable steel for use in making repairs on farm machinery where no spare parts were available from the manufacturers. Most of these manufacturers were producing war equipment—guns, tanks, jeeps, cranes, and other war equipment.

Thomas decided that when George cut up the scrap farm equipment, he needed to save a variety of steel to be sold not as scrap, but items to be used to weld or bolt together a piece of equipment, whatever the customer needed. This variety included: angle Iron, channel Iron, strap iron, pipe, bar iron, plate, boiler flues, and other miscellaneous pieces of steel. He asked George to set the various items aside in an organized manner. Then Thomas began to advertise in the Harriet Press these various steel items.

It was county fair time and Mildred had several things she was going to enter into competition. It was the discussion at the breakfast table on a Saturday morning. Wanda was the first to speak. "What are you entering this year, mother?"

"I have your flowered dress made of feed sacks, 10 different canned vegetables, and 6 canned fruits. Our honeydew melon did not mature in time for the fair. They need another two weeks."

"I have these midway tickets that I would like to use," Wanda said, "but Bruce is on vacation with his parents, so I don't have anyone to go with."

"Isn't one of your other boyfriends available to take you?" Mildred asked. Just then the phone rang in the kitchen and she jumped up to answer it. Wanda sat in silence eating her breakfast. George stopped eating for a few seconds, then spoke.

"Wanda, if you would like, I will go with you to the midway." She never responded to George's invitation. Within 5 minutes Wanda left the table. Mildred returned to finish her breakfast.

"George, did Wanda mention any other boy that could take her to the midway?"

"No, she did not. But I told her that I would take her," he responded.

"And she said what?" Mildred asked.

"She said nothing—she was quiet—then she left."

Chapter 4

Later when Wanda came in with the mail from the mail box, Mildred said to her, "I understand that George offered to take you to the midway."

"He did ask me," Wanda answered. "But I do not want him to take me."

"And why not, Wanda?"

"I am embarrassed to be seen with him. Some of my friends think he is a spy for the Japs. They think that someday he will attack our city with a group of his friends."

"Wanda! That is nonsense. I hope that he didn't hear you say that."

"That is silly," Wanda agreed with a slight laugh. "Maybe I should try to set my friends straight when they tell me that."

"A good idea, Wanda," Mildred also agreed. "One other thing, Wanda, I would prefer that you stop calling George's people Japs. It is an unkind name for them."

Jill Miller was Wanda's best friend. She had never had a chance to meet George and they rarely ran into each other at the Olson household. It was a Tuesday when Jill and George happened to run into each other on the Olson porch. Jill was coming to see if Wanda happened to be home and George came in to make some coffee. "Hi, I'll bet you are George, the new hire of Wanda's father," Jill announced as she was about to knock at the door. "Is Wanda home?"

"No. She and her parents went to the store to get some groceries for her birthday party tomorrow. If you wish to come in, I will make you some coffee," he said.

"I would like that, George," Jill said kindly. He opened the door and let Jill in.

"Have a seat on the sofa and I will make the coffee. Wanda and her folks will be back in about a half hour, if you don't mind waiting."

"Let me ask you a question, if you don't mind, while we are waiting," Jill asked.

"Ask away Jill," George replied. "I'm not sure what I can tell you. I will start the coffee and you ask while I'm making it."

"We are studying Japan in my summer History class. What do you know about the origins of the Japanese people? It is rather strange that we are studying the history of a country that we are at war with, but that is my assignment." George sat down on a chair at the kitchen table and took a deep breathe.

"Short Question—long answer," George replied.

"Look, if you don't have time, you don't have to answer the question," she responded.

"I will take the time," he politely answered. "Here is some paper for you to take notes. If we don't finish before we run out of time, we can finish it some other time. Let me start out by saying that I think it is good that Americans study their enemy for one big reason. The U.S. will win this war and will probably help Japan regain their stature in the world by helping them."

George talked non-stop for the next hour while Jill wrote notes non-stop. Jill had two pages both sides of notes after an hour, and 3 cups of coffee later.

They had just finished when the Olson family came home from shopping. "I just finished listening to an hour lecture by George on the origins of the Japanese people," Jill told Wanda. "He also made me coffee. Thank you George." Wanda stood silent in the kitchen

Chapter 4

while Mildred was putting the groceries away. Both Wanda and Jill walked outside to talk. George started walking back to his room in the tool shed. He passed where Jill and Wanda were standing.

"Jill, are you free to go to the midway tonight?" George asked.

"I am, George," she answered.

"I will pick you up at 6 pm." Wanda remained quiet.

Jill and George had a good time at the midway riding on most of the rides. Later on, they walked over to Jill's home where he met her parents. They had never met him previously and seemed to be impressed with his knowledge on a variety of subjects—especially with the war in the pacific. Jill's mother made a batch of divinity fudge. The parents, along with Jill, and George ate the entire pan of divinity.

On his way home George walked on the Chicago and Northwestern Railroad tracks, taking the shortcut. He practiced balancing by walking on one rail. It was not the safest route to walk because of the vagrants roaming the tracks. As it got darker outside, the numbers of bums, hoboes, and tramps increased. George had heard that this stretch of the railway was not very safe, but he had never experienced the activity before this night. It was scary.

George was very glad that he had heard from his family in California. He just hoped that the authorities never traced the letter back to Harriet. He wondered how the Japanese were being treated in the internment camps. He spent some of his spare time in the newspaper and magazine bins looking for news of the internment camps. Maybe he could find some news of their activities or conditions. Since it was a sensitive subject the government was not very willing to publish much about it. *Maybe in a couple of months I will try to send another letter,* he thought to himself.

One night George had a hard time falling asleep. The trains going past the tool shed were many. He looked outside one time and saw at least 3 troop trains going past to the west not over 10 minutes apart. George figured that some major offensive must be in the works somewhere in the pacific — probably on one of the pacific islands. In addition to the troop trains there were two long freight trains pulled by huge steam engines going each way. Finally, he gave up and forced himself to sleep.

The next morning at breakfast Mildred asked George about his night with Jill. "How was the midway, George?"

"It was perfect," George responded, "it was my first time. I am glad I went." Wanda sat quietly without saying a word. Mildred only stared at Wanda with a look that told her that her difficulty with her was that she refused to go with him to the midway after he had asked her nicely. "Maybe I will do it again sometime. Right now I need to have a date with a cutting torch."

Chapter 4

One of their customers stopped in one morning and had a question for Thomas and Mildred. "I am in a bind. My potatoes have been dug and need to be picked. I have no one to pick them. All of the ladies who are pickers are taken by other potato growers. I don't dare leave the spuds on the ground for long since the forecast is for rain. What should I do?" Thomas took another sip of his coffee, cleared his throat and spoke.

"If three people were to pick and worked hard, how long would it take?"

The potato farmer thought for a few seconds, then answered. "They could do it in 2 days."

"Ok," Thomas said. "Here is what we are going to do. Mildred will stay in the office and tend to business. Wanda, George, and I will pick potatoes at your farm for 2 days. Then, give the money that we earn to Mildred. She will open an account at the bank that will be entitled, 'Food for Hungry Farmers.' We will ask anyone who wishes, to also contribute to the fund. I will find three clergy members in the area to buy food and distribute it in a fair and equitable manner to farmers who need food for their families. I have been searching for an idea for this type of ministry for some time now.

"That is an excellent idea, Thomas," the farmer said. "Let's start picking tomorrow. I will tell the other potato growers the plan and maybe they will also contribute."

The next morning the Olson family was up early, packed a lunch, and drove 10 miles to where they would pick potatoes for the next two days. The decision that needed to be made was who would pick with who? Wanda did not desire to pick alongside George. All of them knew this. "How about if we draw straws," Thomas suggested. "I will make 3 sticks and we will each pick one. The longest stick gets to pick who he or she will pick potatoes with. The third person picks by him or herself." The result was that George picked by himself.

During the two days of picking, a total of $55 was earned. The farmer gave Mildred the cash plus $20 for a total of $75. It was the start of the food fund for the struggling farmers.

Since it was getting close to winter, George and Thomas thought it would be best to begin getting ready for the trapping season. The two managers had not had time to prepare for this important time of the year for many of the farmers. They had been busy in the surplus gathering activities. Wisconsin was one of the best fur states because of three reasons, 1—it had many bodies of water, 2—there were many wooded areas, and 3—field corn and sweet corn was a major food for many of the fur bearing animals.

Because of the war on two fronts, the demand for the fur skins was high. Thomas had traveled to Brooklyn where a fur manufacturing plant was all set up and ready to go. They would make fur pelts into pilot helmets and vests. A processing shack was set up several hundred feet from where the Olson house was located to prevent the smell from getting too close.

The carcasses would be ground into meat scraps for extra profit, some of which were worth a higher price than other scraps. The fat was sold for use in making explosives. Thomas and George were faced with the task of finding labor for the processing jobs. A list of high school students was obtained from the high school principal. The

Chapter 4

one requirement was that the student needed to have a 'B' average or above. Since no one had any experience, Thomas offered to give any who wished to train a dollar per hour for the first 8 hours on a Saturday. Anyone could quit the job at any time, and would get paid if they could not stand the smell or the job.

All during the training period, Wanda could not stand the smell of the animals. George stayed in the tool shed almost the entire trapping season. He took a hot shower each night. After the Saturday afternoon shower, he took another shower in the house to make sure he was absolutely clean for Sunday. George was so dressed up and clean on the first Sunday morning that Wanda didn't recognize him right away. "I am supposed to invite you over for dinner," she said to George.

"Thank you," George answered kindly.

During the worship service, George almost had the intestinal fortitude to sit down by Wanda. She was sitting alone. As he was about to make his move, he decided to scrap the idea.

It had been many years since the area around Harriet had a fur season so that the game warden needed to have a training session with the trappers. Many of the regular trappers were off to war. Many of the game wardens were also off to war. Game wardens used the laws to control the populations of animals. The state had, in the years past, implemented a means of making sure that over-the-limit amount had not been taken by the trappers. Because no seasons had been held for years during the depression, many of the animal populations had gotten out of hand. It appeared that this fall there was going to be a bumper year for almost all of the fur-bearing animals.

This would be the first year in 10 years that there was going to be a season on beaver. Some type of disease had stricken the beaver about 10 years previously. For each beaver that was taken during this first year, the trapper was given $.25 cents per pound by the Olson Fur Company. When the beaver was skinned and stretched out, this was the approximate value that the Olson Fur Company could pay and still make a profit. Unfortunately, George discovered one evening that some trappers were melting and pouring hot lead down the dead beaver's throat to add more weight. Thomas called the authorities and they put a stop to that.

There was an art to processing the beaver from the dead animal to the dried round skin ready for tanning at the fur manufacturer. Because the war had taken from Harriet one of the best persons in this art, Thomas thought he would not be able to take off running with the beaver business. Fortunately, an American Indian who came home from the war to visit his uncle in Harriet, Wisconsin happened to be well experienced in processing beaver. He was taught by his Grandfather at his boyhood home in North Dakota. He spent 2 days training George on this art before the soldier had to return to his station where he was a Wind Talker—using his native language to send messages to the American troops. The Japanese had a difficult time understanding the codes in the Lakota language.

A problem that was occurring with the fox was when the game warden would tag each fox. Because of the damage the fox were costing the farmers, the trappers were given $1 for each one in

Chapter 4

addition to what they got for the fur. The game warden would snip off the front paws. Three counties away the game warden would snip off the back paws, making it possible for some of the crooked trappers to collect double the bounty. They just had to travel to the next county. That soon stopped.

Probably the worst deception leveled against the Olson Fur Company was with the valuable fur animal, mink. They were very valuable, especially the males. They were worth up to $10 more than the females. Their fur is better and they are larger. But what happens when a very large female is caught in a trap? The unscrupulous trapper had that situation all figured out. The trapper will skin the mink and then stretch it on a wooden stretcher. Once it is dry, he would light up a cigarette and carefully burn a spot on the female skin where the male sex organ would appear. When the fur buyer sees the female skin he is tricked into thinking it is a male mink. Fortunately, the perpetrators were caught at this fraudulent practice early on.

The War Emergency Board of the fur industry, in December 1942, held a fur contribution drive to aid in the shortage of fur material to make fur-lined vests and helmets for pilots. To facilitate this collection drive, many communities in the country held a "Fur Ball." Admission to the ball was by means of the donation of a piece of fur clothing. Service men and woman home on leave were admitted free. All other persons were charged $.75 contribution.

The Olson family was in the kitchen one morning when Thomas was expected to make his appearance to eat with them. He came rushing in with pain and agony and holding a big live male mink. "This mink who I thought was dead came to life again and bit my hand around the thumb as I opened up the trunk. He has locked on and will not let go. They clamp on to their victim like a pit bull and suck the blood." Wanda quickly left the table and ran to the bathroom where she lost her cookies. "I have tried everything to get him to let go—but he won't."

Mildred happened to have a 10 gallon copper boiler full of water on the stove. She was boiling the water for washing clothes. As luck would have it the water was almost at the point of boiling. Mildred grabbed Thomas' hand along with his arm and the mink and dunked them into the boiling water. The mink immediately let go and Thomas threw him into a burlap bag for later processing. Quickly he pulled his hand and arm out of the water. He ran into the bathroom where he ran warm and hot water into the mink bite and washed it out well. Wanda treated the bite with some whiskey from the prohibition days and then wrapped it good. "Thank you nurse," Thomas said.

Wanda was doing well with her studies at the college she was attending. Her plans were to go to work part-time at a hospital working in the maternity ward. She also had an interest in marrying a doctor or lawyer after she had worked a few years in nursing. These plans, however, were not in total agreement with her parent's wishes. They wanted her to become a missionary nurse. Wanda rejected this plan and did not even want to talk about it with her parents. Her

Chapter 4

parents knew of course it was a decision she was someday going to make herself, hopefully with the guidance of the Lord.

Wanda brought home a guest one weekend to meet the family. He was a student in medicine at the school he was attending. It was in the same county as the school where Wanda was attending. Both of them had decided to attend college year-round, in order to complete their education as soon as possible. Wanda did not inform her parents that she was bringing this doctor student home for the weekend. In addition, no plans were made as to where the doctor student would be housed. They drove into the driveway at about 3 p.m.

When she started college, she received permission to invite a friend home sometime as long as she informed her mother of the invite ahead of time.

"Mom and Dad, I would like you to meet James Mason. He and I have worked together at a hospital near where I go to school." The Olson's were slightly annoyed by their daughter's surprise guest and his sudden introduction. "This is my father Thomas, and this is my mother Mildred," Wanda continued.

"Come right in and sit down. Make yourself comfortable," Mildred replied. They all sat quietly for a few seconds not knowing exactly what to do. Finally, Mildred stood up and motioned for Wanda to come to the kitchen. Mildred spoke silently to Wanda, "Wanda, what is going on?"

"You said one time that I could bring a friend home from college—so here he is." Wanda uttered this in a weak voice knowing that her mother did not approve of what she did. At the same time, she suddenly recalled that her mother had asked her to inform her when she did make the invite.

"Tell me, Wanda, where is he going to sleep, or is he planning on driving back to school tonight?"

"I thought he could sleep in one of our guest rooms," Wanda answered.

"Wanda, this is all wrong. What are we going to feed him? Will he go to church with us? Who will chaperone you two?"

Mildred and Thomas decided to make the best of a very uncomfortable situation and welcome their uninvited guest as an invited guest. A problem came up when George walked into the house for supper. Wanda had forgotten about him. She had never told her new friend about George. George knew that Wanda was ashamed of him and would just as soon not have him in the same room when she was there.

The supper meal was good, with steak, baked potatoes, carrots, homemade bread, and dessert. George realized the difficulty of the situation and orchestrated the conversation so that everyone had a good time. The topics included the war, the doctor's work, Wanda's schooling, and ending with George telling about bumming a freight. The time around the table lasted almost 2 hours. During that time Mildred and Wanda figured out where the doctor was going to sleep.

Later that night, Mildred had some strong words with Wanda concerning the entire episode. "Wanda, tell me, what did this ordeal reveal tonight?"

"I do not know," she answered. "What?"

"It showed that George has abilities and talents that make him a very fine individual and you need to take note of them and him."

CHAPTER 5

There were many times that customers attempted to take advantage of the Olson Iron and Metal Company with dishonest transactions. Most of these involved dishonest, inaccurate, crooked, or criminal practices. Mildred, Thomas, and George were all on the constant lookout for where and when they would occur. One would think that coming off of the depression, people would try to be as honest as possible. Most were—some were not

One of these practices was stealing scrap iron and metal from the scrap yard during the night and then selling it back during the daytime hours. This was not very easy to do since the items stolen were mostly recognizable. Thomas and George had an eagle eye for recognizing items bought just days before, items that they would see every day, or items that had an unusual feature. The gate on the road going into the Olson Scrap Yard was usually locked at night making it difficult to access items to steal. It was sometimes rather noisy when the perpetrators were stealing steel with the noisy steam engines rumbling by the scrap yard. The noise made it easy to hide the racket made by the people stealing.

When there were no trains going past, the pieces that were being stolen would clang and bang together. The noise would usually wake the Olson family up especially during the evening hours and at night.

Sometimes the thieves would break down the fence or hacksaw the chain holding the lock or locks. Occasionally, the really ambitious scoundrels would lift or throw the scrap over the wooden fence. Then where would they haul it to? Where would they park their trailer or hayrack? They sometimes did not think of that.

Even though it was on the tail end of the depression it still was worth the risk of getting caught and thrown in jail for a few days. To many of the railroad bums it was their objective to get caught and be thrown into the local jail for a free bed and food.

George was instrumental in keeping the losses from stolen steel to a minimum. He did this by keeping the hauled-in farm machinery cut up into prepared steel for the steel mills. If a customer drove in with a trunk full of scrap that was obviously cut up with a torch, it was a dead giveaway as to where it came from. Added to the torch cuts were George's unique torch cuts. It happened on two occasions where Thomas was able to catch the offenders attempting to sell steel cut by George a few days before. Thomas got the customer to admit that he had walked into the scrap yard from the back fence and carried the steel one mile to his car. "You must have been really hungry," George told the guy.

Thomas told the customer to back his car up to the railroad car that was being loaded and throw the stolen steel into it. When asked by Thomas why he did it, the customer said that his family was hungry. That afternoon Thomas had Mildred drive to the man's home with a box full of basic food items.

Chapter 5

The people who were most likely to steal were the bums, tramps, and hobos from along the railroad tracks. They knew what items in the junk yard were of the most value and if successful in stealing would aid them in purchasing a glass or bottle of booze. Sometimes a construction company would leave electrical wire or cooper tubing lying at a construction site and find it missing the next morning. If someone stole a roll of wire with the insulation still on it, they would find a dump ground or out of the way location and burn it off. They knew how to burn it just right, so that they didn't get the wire too hot. The wire could oxidize to the point where some of the weight may go out of the wire.

Another item that was often stolen, worth a great amount of money, and easy to obtain were the red brass journals on railroad car axle boxes. They were filled with old rags and oil. If one or more of the eight axle boxes on the cars were not filled with oil, the box surrounding the axle would get hot to the point where the box would start on fire. The Babbitt would melt and cause the car to malfunction and could cause a derailment of the train.

When the repair crew would fix the hotbox, the two brass journals would be tossed on the ground next to the tracks. Someone would see them, pick them up and sell them to a nearby scrap metal dealer. Since they were red brass they were worth up to $1.50, depending on the price of red brass at the time. The people who took them were stealing railroad property and the scrap yard buying the journals were buying stolen property.

In addition to the red brass journals, the lead that dripped out of the hot box was sometimes picked up by the hobos, tramps, or bums and also sold to the local scrap metal buyer. Usually the tramp would collect a sack full before selling it since the Babbitt from one hot box did not amount to much weight. The money was usually spent on liquor or sometimes on food.

One local bum's father was killed in WW I in Europe and the son inherited thousands. He spent most of the money on liquor and buying moonshine to the point where the locals called him Mooney. Mildred always felt sorry for Mooney and would often give him a loaf of homemade bread when he came to sell a few pounds of metal.

It was a struggle for the three principals of the business to strike a happy medium between giving food to those who really needed it and those who would grab anything they could and sell it to their buddies.

George continued to dig up the 'gold mines' as he called them, on the far outer edge of the Olson Scrap Yard. It was where the floor sweepings were dumped during the middle 1930s when nonferrous metal was low in price. He would sort the bits of metal out into gallon cans and sell it back to the firm when the cans were filled. Since George did not have much to spend the money on, he would deposit it in the State Bank of Harriet, along with his weekly check from the business that Mildred would give him. He also placed a tithe in the offering every Sunday at church—a practice he had learned from his parents.

One day a customer came in with a 5-gallon pail full of razor blades. Thomas and George thought it was a bit unusual for someone to collect that many razor blades into a pail. Thomas thought he

Chapter 5

should ask the man the reason. "Sir, if I may ask you, where did you get all of those razor blades?" The man who had a beard and didn't seem to be shaving it, gave out a slight laugh, then answered.

"I expected you to ask that question," he responded unashamedly. "I am from the town in the next county and we just celebrated our 75th year anniversary. A contest was held to see who could shave the fastest. It was a big mistake. If you look closely, you will see that some of the blades have blood on them. Almost every contestant cut themselves. We have only one doctor in town and we had to bring in doctors from other towns. A couple men cut their throats a little. Never will we do that again. A new razor blade was used for each man, and when each man was done, the used blade was thrown into the 5-gallon pail."

From the start of the scrap collection drive, many farmers were bringing in cattle bones. They ranged from just butchered and cleaned off bones to those picked off of the pastures where the animal had died and the birds had picked them clean. Most were cattle bones, but some were bones of other critters. Many still had the animal flesh on them which made for a very stinky situation. Thomas needed to place a note in the Harriet Press that read "Only cleaned off bones will be accepted—Let the dogs clean the bones."

At the supper table one evening, Wanda asked an interesting question. "Why would the government want those smelly old bones?" Thomas had the answer.

"Bones are made into glue for airplane construction as well as being used in munitions during the War. Horse hoofs are usually used for glue but since horses are no longer used like in WW I, they need to use any bones."

When the first boxes of old rags came in, there was a new kind of problem facing the Olson's—rather it was a new opportunity, as pointed out by George.

Many of the rags were almost new clothes. Both Thomas and Mildred saw an opportunity. Many of the people who had struggled through the depression did so with a lack of good fitting clothes. They decided to organize a group from their church to sort through the old clothes and pick out those that could be given to people who could use them. There was an empty room in the church basement that was converted into a used clothing store.

Many of the citizens of Harriet had more nice clothes than they needed. The call for collecting surplus clothes reminded them that they had too much and this would be an excuse to get rid of these clothes and thereby rid themselves of guilt.

It was decided to charge a nominal fee for the clothes. The reason? Since the church basement store was so close to the railroad tracks, it would be easy for the 'men and women of the tracks' to walk in and select free clothes, sell them to their buddies on the other side of the tracks, and go to the nearest downtown bar for refreshments.

Waste paper was also collected for use in the war effort. The need for paper begin very soon after Pearl Harbor mainly because laborers who normally cut the pulpwood were enlisting or were being drafted into the various military services. Afraid that the pulp and paper industry may shutdown, the U.S. Government informed the public

Chapter 5

and voluntary salvage committees of the severe shortage, immediate and potential.

Many thousands of pounds of scrap paper were used for packing military shells alone. The military use of paper milk bottles were required. Blue print paper was needed to draw the plans for each new battleship.

The response was overwhelming since there was vast quantities of scrap paper sitting everywhere—in closets, basements, garages, and in attics. Coming out of a depression, most people were used to not throwing anything away.

There was an upcoming party at church for which George wanted to find a date. He had never asked Wanda out in his time at the Olson home. *Would she go with him?* He wondered. He had overheard Thomas and Mildred talk about that possibility at least 3 times. It was time to ask.

Two days later Wanda was walking past where George was cutting steel with the cutting torch. He noticed her walking towards him. He shut off the torch and prepared to ask her. "Wanda, may I ask you a question?"

"Yes you may," she said in a slightly non interested manner. She was suspecting that George was going to ask her that very question.

"The church is having a mission's benefit party two weeks from Friday night. It's a basket social party. I have never been to one. Would you be so kind as to accompany me? It's where the girls invite the men."

"I <u>know</u> what it is," she answered in a superior tone. Wanda just looked at George and said "Maybe," and walked on. George did not know what to think. He couldn't take a chance and needed to know her decision. He needed to make sure the suit that was given him fit. He needed to get a haircut, and he needed to ask Thomas if he could use the family car. Mildred was asked to provide a picnic basket in case an extra one was needed. It was the girls who provided the picnic basket and the boys or men who did the bidding.

George asked Mildred if she would help iron his suit and shirt, and suggest a flower to give his date. "I will be glad to do those things for you," Mildred answered. "It appears that you are going on a date."

"Hopefully, Mildred, keep tuned," he hinted. Apparently Mildred then talked to Thomas. Later that night Thomas walked up to George and gave him a set of keys.

"Here George, use this car on your date, it is in the garage in the trees in back. Go out and look at it."

George immediately walked into the woods, opened the door of the garage, turned on the light, and almost fell over. There in front of him was a bright shiny green 1928 Buick Road master. He opened the front car door and crawled in the driver's seat. *"But what happens if Wanda says 'no',"* he said out loud.

Another item that people were getting involved with was oil and kitchen fat. In 1942 the main supply of vegetable oil was disrupted by the war in the Pacific. This product was in great demand for glyceride that was needed in making explosives. The housewives in America saved the fat that came off of many of the cuts of meat from hogs,

Chapter 5

beef, sheep, and poultry. Since it wasn't very long after the depression, most of the housewives were conditioned to saving the fat in 5-gallon lard tins. Many women made their own soap using this fat. The Olson family had made their soap for at least 10 years. Another component of soap was lye.

Nearly 350 pounds of fat was needed to fire one shell from a 12-inch naval gun. Three pounds of fat will provide enough glycerin to make a pound of gunpowder. Until Pearl Harbor approximately 60 % of the glycerin used in the United States had been obtained from fats and oils imported from the pacific areas, most of which were now under the control of the Japanese.

Many churches became involved with the scrap and salvage drives across the nation. It provided a patriotic purpose where various groups within the church could gather.

The lack of workers during the war became a challenge for many industries and businesses. Women needed to fill in, in order to maintain the commerce. It was very quickly realized that the women could produce as well as, and in some cases, even better than their male counterparts. For example, women seem to have better depth perception than men. Therefore, they made better forklift drivers than men.

Rubber became scarce when supplies from the Dutch East Indies were no longer available due to Japan controlling that area. Community groups were urged to bring old tires, old bathing caps, rubber trunk mats, rubber soles and heels that were worn out, and anything rubber.

The Harriet Theater conducted a promotion whereby they would give a free admission for either a half pound of scrap copper or 25 pounds of steel.

Women were asked to turn in their hosiery to help with the war effort. Silk stockings were used to make powder bags in naval and artillery guns, while nylon hose was used to manufacture parachute and tow ropes for gliders. In one instance a woman in Harriet who had been making rugs from old stockings brought in her finished rugs, while another woman donated 118 pairs of stockings she had collected over a period of 10 years intending to make rugs.

It was becoming harder and harder to keep the vagrants and drifters from stealing the more valuable metal from the scrap yard. Thomas and George attempted to keep the non-ferrous metal inside of the main shop building. The would-be crooks seemed to know where the valuable metals were kept. The answer was to get a guard dog.

Mildred's brother had a fine purebred female German shepherd who recently had a litter of puppies. Thomas asked Mildred who should be the one to pick out the puppy that would grow up to be a good guard dog. "Should it be Wanda or George? Let's ask them if either of them would want to pick. Let's see what they would say," Mildred responded.

"I will present it to them at supper tonight. According to my brother, we have a pick from 3 females and 3 males—various color combinations."

At supper that evening Thomas presented the challenge to the two teenagers. They both agreed to decide who would pick. George then spoke up to the wonder of Wanda. "Let me interject something here, if I could." Wanda rolled her eyes as if to say, *I'll bet he's going to pull rank and will want the choice to be exclusively his.*

Chapter 5

"My experience has been that women pick the best," George continued. "They have an uncanny way of sensing the puppy with the best characteristics—male or female. So I think Wanda should do the picking." Everyone sat quietly at the table not expecting George's words. "However, I would like to go with you to the farm to see all of the puppies".

George drove the car and Wanda rode along to her uncle's farm to pick out a German shepherd puppy. When they walked into the barn the sound of puppy noise filled the air. "These puppies come from good breeding stock," George stated, "I can tell by how they try to get our attention. "Wanda, you are going to have a hard time choosing."

"I know George," she responded. "This will take some time."

"Well, just take your time. It's important that we get it right."

Wanda handled each puppy for a few minutes. Then she picked out 3—2 females and 1 male. She then looked into each puppie's eyes for a full minute. She finally settled on the dark brown female puppy and rubbed noses with her. From there they went to the car and took off for home. "Thank you Wanda for doing this. Maybe you should write a book on 'How to pick the best dog out of a litter of puppies.'" Wanda seemed to appreciate the compliment from George.

When they arrived home the family had a discussion about naming the puppy. Mildred had the first suggestion. "If it was a boy puppy we could name it Max."

"How about naming the puppy Maxine," George suggested.

"Sounds great—Maxine it is," Thomas added.

The puppy Maxine started out as a favorite with everyone in the family. Normally, it took several days to train a puppy to do what the master wants him or her to do. In this case, all the family wanted him to do was to let someone know when a stranger was roaming around the scrap yard. George had a book that he found in the books donated, entitled, 'Training a Dog in the Art of Guarding'.

In two weeks Wanda came home for a day from college as it was a holiday. At the breakfast table George asked Wanda if she could help him with a task. "What do you have for me to do?" she asked.

"Will you please help me train Maxine?" George asked.

"Don't you think Maxine is a little young for training?" Wanda responded.

"On the contrary—I say start them young."

"OK, if you say so."

Both of them took Maxine out to the property in the scrap yard where they taught her to "come", to "sit", and to "bark." They used a bag of steak treats as rewards. It took only three hours to accomplish these commands.

"This afternoon we will teach Maxine to warn us when something unusual appears in the yard. That's if you are free this afternoon."

"I am free until 4 p.m.," Wanda replied.

During the lunch hour Maxine was sitting outside by the house when all of a sudden she began to bark loudly at something unusual. Wanda got up from the table and walked outside. A tramp from the railroad tracks was walking toward the house. Maxine ran close to the tramp and the tramp stopped. He then turned around and hurried

Chapter 5

out of the property. "Maxine has learned how to scare danger off of our property," Wanda informed everyone.

After lunch, the two dog trainers continued their training of Maxine in various tricks. At 4 p.m. it was time for Wanda to go back to school. "Thank you for helping me to train our puppy, Wanda," George said as he smiled at Wanda, "Have a good week in school."

The following Sunday afternoon an accident occurred on the Chicago and Northwestern Railroad on the East-bound tracks going through Harriet. It could have been very tragic had it been at night, had the train been traveling faster, and had a rail been broken much worse. A 12-car troop train was traveling east at a speed of 40 miles per hour when a cracked rail broke into 3 pieces just in back of the 2 steam engines, causing the engines to travel on. The 12 cars broke off, jumped the tracks it was on and continued to travel on in between the two sets of tracks. As the cars were filled with sailors, soldiers, marines, and government personnel, they all got out of the cars as soon as possible.

The Olson family heard the train breakup and immediately knew what the tragedy was. Thomas ran outside and on to the driveway which crosses the tracks. He could see the 2 steam engines as they traveled fast to the next town for help. Thomas ran back to the house and quickly called the local depot agent to inform him of the accident. "Tell the railroad to send at least 10 coaches to pick up the stranded military personnel. Also, send medical personnel to treat the injured."

Mildred immediately set to work making sandwiches and coffee for the soldiers. Thomas began to call the cafés and bars and asked them to bring over food. He figured that some of the military personnel would very quickly find out that the bars were open on Sunday in Wisconsin, but could not sell liquor.

The railroad repair crew was called and were on their way to the derailment sight within one hour. Since it was one of the main East-West rail lines, the military became very much involved with the repair work. For security reasons news of the accident was not circulated, even to the local newspaper. At first the investigators said the accident looked very much like sabotage. They even roamed on the roads through the scrap yard searching for any evidence.

Thomas called the various churches in Harriet asking if they would be willing to bring food and coffee over to feed the stranded soldiers. He also called the doctors in town asking them if they could come and check out any injuries that may have occurred with the boys and women. Some of the women on the train were nurses who went right into action.

The next morning George spent most of his time using the torch to cut up twisted rails. A steam driven railroad crane lifted the coach and Pullman cars off the roadbed and onto the westbound track. The rails were then cut into 36" long pieces and piled up out of the way. Thomas talked to the Road-master of the railroad and made an agreement where he would keep the scrap rails in exchange for letting them dump them on his land.

There was a total of one mile of track that was scrapped totaling 228 tons of #1 steel. Since rails are made of a special kind of steel, the price that it would bring for scrap per ton would be more than normal. The road master told Thomas that the railroad would let his company have this steel for 4 reasons: (1) For the disruption to their business, (2) for keeping the press out, (3) for keeping people from taking photos, and (4) for organizing a quick reaction to the accident.

Chapter 5

Within two days the rail bed was back in use. For the next three days there was a continuous chain of backed up troop and military trains travelling slowly through Harriet playing catchup.

It was now the day of the Basket Social at the Harriet Bible Church. Wanda had still not communicated with George as to her decision to go with him. He was losing hope. Mildred and Thomas somehow knew about the proposed date but chose to stay clear of any involvement. They wanted to be free of any unwanted influence on behalf of either of the two young people. Mildred and Thomas were, however, providing some items for George—Mildred helping with the clothes and Thomas with a car.

Wanda did tell her mother earlier in the week that she was planning on going, but not with what person. The usual procedure for this church basket social was that a girl or woman would prepare a picnic basket and the boys or men would bid on the baskets. The winner of the basket (boy or man) would then have the opportunity to eat the contents of the basket with the provider (girl or woman). In order for the evening to be fair and equitable, there needed to be some horse trading involved. There also needed to be as many baskets provided from females as there were males participating.

Things started happening about 5 pm when Wanda came home from visiting her friend Jill Miller. She quietly got dressed and took off in her car. She never told anyone where she was going. As she walked through the kitchen, she couldn't help but notice the freshly pressed suit and white shirt of George's hanging on the back of a chair. She left a note on the table for George. The note read—*'George,*

Sorry, you will need to attend the basket social by yourself. I have a previous engagement.—Wanda.'

George quickly got dressed, backed the 1928 Buick Road master out of the garage, drove over to the church, and walked in. Mildred spotted him right away looking rather sad. She knew right away the problem and tried to console him.

"That's ok, Mom, I will just be patient. Someday I will win." Mildred then gave him a hug. He spent the rest of the night bidding on baskets in a crafty manner, such that the prices were jacked up on most everything. George was the high bidder on three different baskets. He ate a portion of each with 3 different individuals. The remainder he carried back to his tool shed home and placed in his ice box for later consumption. As a result the mission fund had its most profitable basket social ever.

When Wanda arrived home after midnight from wherever she had been, Mildred went to Wanda's bedroom and talked sternly to her. "Wanda, you need to start developing some common courtesy to George. If you don't want to go on a date with him, tell him when he asks you. Don't leave him hanging."

"Ok Mom, I'm sorry, I'll try to do that."

"Don't express your regret to me, Wanda, express it to George.

CHAPTER 6

July of 1944

Wanda was home after her first full year at college. She was enrolled in the school of nursing at a hospital college about 50 miles from Harriet. One of her classes allowed her to do some of the work by correspondence during the summer and obtain 5 credit hours. She would be able to live at home, thus saving some money by not having to pay for dorm rent at college. In addition, her father offered her work in the scrap yard doing miscellaneous odd jobs.

George did not mind seeing Wanda around the scrap yard as he was very fond of her beauty. He would often fantasize a relationship with her someday in the future. However, he had made up his mind to keep a social distance from her, to maintain respect and honor with both her and her parents. Most of all, he made it his personal goal to protect her from any unsavory men who walked and rode the rails. He had promised Thomas that he would be Wanda's secret body guard. At the same time both Thomas and Mildred realized what was going on in George's mind with their daughter. They often discussed it and thought it may be an acceptable thing if someday the two would date and maybe get married. During such discussions the question of a mixed racial marriage was brought up. Both of Wanda's parents came from an upbringing that taught that it was probably questionable for one race of people to marry another race,—even part racial. It was not forbidden, only that, down the road, there may be some potential social difficulties with such a union involving the offspring. The subject was never discussed when Wanda was anywhere in the listening vicinity. Both Wanda and George were aware of the need for a couple to be equally yoked spiritually even more importantly than having the same social and cultural interests.

Wanda's parents did see a potential problem with both Wanda and George living and working so close together in the same group of buildings and eating at the same table. So far in the two years that George had been with the Olson's, their daughter and George had not been on a formal date. "This could happen this summer," Mildred said to Thomas as they were sitting drinking coffee at the kitchen table the second night that Wanda was home from school. "They both will be attending the same youth group at church, I presume," Thomas said. "That means they will be riding in the same car, going to social gatherings together, and communicating, hopefully."

"What about Bruce, her boyfriend through high school, or maybe some boys she has met at college during the year?" Thomas asked Mildred.

"When I asked her about that topic, she is quiet," Mildred replied. "She is very set in pursuing a career in nursing at her college. She has an application in at our local hospital for a part-time nurse's aide job this summer."

Three days after Wanda arrived home from college she decided to go for a walk along the railroad tracks. As she was walking, she

Chapter 6

passed where George was junking an old International tractor for its scrap iron. "Hi George," Wanda surprised him.

"Hi Wanda," George returned her greeting. It was then that he noticed her attire. It was a swimsuit that revealed Wanda's' beauty as never seen by George. *What is she trying to do?* He asked himself. *Walking alone in a bathing suit on the railroad track with all of the hobos, tramps, and bums. She is asking for trouble.* She kept walking another half mile, turned around, walked past George once again, and then walked back to the house. George suddenly became worried about her. With all of the sexually hungry males roaming the tracks, her safety, and welfare could be in trouble. George thought further—maybe she was trying only to tease me.

That afternoon, George was in the kitchen for a 3 p.m. coffee break. Mildred was sitting on the opposite end of the table reading a magazine. "Mildred, may I interrupt your concentration to talk about something that I think is very important concerning Wanda?"

"Go ahead and speak, George," she responded. "She is at a friend's house right now."

"Here is my concern about Wanda," he began. "As you are aware, I am very fond of her. She is almost like a sister to me. I would give my life to protect her from anyone attempting to hurt her. This morning I saw her walking alone on the railroad tracks in a bathing suit that made her look almost as good as the Betty Grable photo that all the GI's are hanging up in their tents and foxholes. She is asking for trouble, with all of the strange men roaming the tracks." Mildred set aside her magazine and looked straight at George.

"I have never heard you talk about Wanda like that before, and you sound very serious. I guess I have never noticed how she dresses lately. Maybe I need to look more closely."

"I need to tell you something," George said with a whispered tone of voice. "When I rode the freight from the west coast to Harriett two years ago, there was an incident that occurred on the train inside the boxcar that I was on. Two young women were riding with the group of men I was standing with. Suddenly two of the men each grabbed one of the women, dragged them to the other end of the boxcar, where it was dark, proceeded to pull off their clothes, and rape them. I felt terrible because I never lifted a finger to help the two ladies. Their screams were terrible."

"George, I am so glad that you told me this," Mildred responded. "I will talk to Wanda about this matter."

"She may get angry at me for talking to you, but I don't care," George commented. "She needs to be warned."

"I will do that," Mildred answered. "Wanda has been participating in theater at college and thinks that she may have a future in acting. She also wants to be the Homecoming Queen at her college in her senior year. Thomas and I think that her future is in nursing. What she is doing, of course, is exhibiting her beauty. That is probably the reason for her wearing those clothes."

The next day Wanda walked past George in the scrap yard. There was a dirty look from her to him. Their eyes met. He then knew that Mildred had talked to Wanda about her attire in and along the railroad tracks. George expected this reaction from her. Once they had passed each other, Wanda turned around and spoke in harsh words: "George, it is none of your damn business what I wear or where I wear it. So, stay out of it." George was expecting these words and the anger

Chapter 6

in which they were expressed. He said nothing, only turned around, closed his eyes, and stood in silence as she walked away.

It was only two weeks after Mildred had spoken to Wanda about wearing more modest clothes that a tragic incidence took place. Wanda's friend, Jill Miller, came over to the Olson house at around 3 p.m. on a Saturday. Her knock at the door brought Mildred out of the guest bedroom where she was cleaning. "Jill, it's good to see you. I bet you are looking for Wanda."

"Yes." Jill spoke up with a surprised look on her face. "She was supposed to come over to my house at 1 p.m.—she never showed."

"You're kidding," Mildred answered in surprise. "She went walking along the railroad track right after lunch. Go ask George if he has seen her." As Mildred finished saying those words, a cold chill entered her body. She recalled her talk with George some two weeks previously. She suddenly recalled her talk with Wanda about the wearing of revealing clothes.

Jill went outside and walked fast down the old road alongside the railroad tracks. She finally saw George beyond the wooden snow fence about a block away. He was using the cutting torch to cut up a load of farm machinery that Thomas had bought the day before. She climbed on to the wooden railroad snow fence and begin waving with both hands to George. After a couple minutes, he saw her waving, shut off his torch and listened closely to Jill. Normally, because of train noise, it would be almost impossible to hear except for short distances. However, this day the noise level and atmosphere was such that George had very little difficulty in hearing sound. He saw that it was Jill on the fence. He put down the torch head, shut off the gas tanks, and ran to the fence. "What's up Jill?" he asked.

"Wanda never showed up at my house at 1 p.m.—her mom said she went for a walk at about 10:30."

"Where did her mother say she went for a walk?" George asked.

"Along the railroad tracks," Jill responded. George froze!

"Oh no! No!! No!!!" George shouted in response, with increasing intensity. He quickly began running toward the Olson house, leaving Jill to walk back alone. He ran into the house and yelled for Mildred. She came running from the back porch.

"George," she spoke in a fearful sound. "What is the matter?"

"Where is Wanda?" George also asked excitedly and with fear. Mildred looked at George and suddenly realized what may have happen to Wanda.

"She went walking on the tracks again," Mildred answered. "But that was hours ago. She never came home for lunch—she was supposed to go to Jill's for lunch. Guess what? Jill just told me that she has been waiting for a couple of hours at her place for Wanda."

"Mildred, I am going to go find Wanda," George said with a shaky voice. Mildred could see that George was visibly shaken by the disappearance of Wanda.

"Where are you going to look?" She asked.

"I will start where she usually starts her walks—where our driveway crosses the tracks." Mildred suddenly began to cry. "Mildred, I need you to call Thomas and the sheriff. Tell them that Wanda is missing and I am going to look for her. Something has happened to her. I know it. Jill, you can walk with me along the tracks and look for anything that will give some clues. Where is Maxine, the puppy dog?"

"She is by the road," Mildred replied.

Chapter 6

"I will use Maxine to help us find Wanda," George said. "Where is Wanda's scarf?" Mildred grabbed a scarf off of a hanger on the kitchen wall and gave it to George. "Once we give Wanda's scent to Maxine, she should be able to find the trail."

George, Jill, and Maxine walked for only a quarter mile when they came upon a partial roll of tape that was laying in the grass. "Someone has abducted Wanda and probably used the tape to tape her mouth shut and bind her hands," George shouted. "Whoever did this was intending on raping Wanda.

"Wherever they did this, they most likely left her lay," George said. "She is close by. I can feel it. Quickly Jill, let's look in these weeds." George let Maxine smell the scent from the roll of tape. "Maxine, go find Wanda! Go find Wanda!!" Maxine took off across the tracks to the other side and began looking and smelling the weeds and under growth.

Both Jill and George began to look feverishly in the weeds by and along the tracks. After searching for a half hour, Jill suddenly yelled from across the tracks.

"George," Jill yelled, "let's listen for sounds of her crying or moaning. It should be easy to hear. There is not much noise"

"Good idea, Jill," George responded. He immediately began to pray out loud.

"Lord, you know where Wanda is. Help us to find her." He was in a hurry. He didn't even have time to say Amen.

They both searched both sides of the tracks for a good ½ mile going east out of Harriet. Nothing. Then suddenly Maxine came upon a gully that usually was filled up with water. He jumped down and licked Wanda's cheek. George looked closely into the gully and could see part of a naked body with a torn garment that looked like

Wanda's swimsuit. He yelled across the tracks. "Jill, run back to the house and tell Mildred to call the police and ambulance. I think Maxine and I have found Wanda." Jill took off as fast as she could, running back toward the house.

George carefully lifted himself down into the gully being careful not to step on Wanda. She was bleeding from the lower part of her body. George took off his blue work shirt and pressed it against the area where the bleeding was coming from. Wanda was also shaking, although George didn't know what that was caused by. He needed to get her out of the gully. He picked her up carefully with one arm around her head and shoulders and the other arm around her naked legs. It was the first time he had ever touched her skin. They had never even shaken hands—not even when they first met in the Olson kitchen. Wanda was 5:10 and to lift her out of the gully took all of the might George could assemble because of where he was standing. He prayed as he maneuvered up the side of the gully.

Lord, you need to help me get us out of this pit. Wanda needs blood fast and medical attention. Speed medical help to us and be with Wanda's parents. Give me extra strength to lift us out of this gully.

Soon the two of them were on the tracks. George placed his mouth next to Wanda's ear. "Wanda, hang in there, we will get you to the hospital very soon."

"George," Wanda whispered gently and brokenly, "I am so sorry I did not listen to you."

"Just remain as still as you can," George responded. "Tell me, how many men attacked you?"

"Two," she spoke, "one with a red coat," and then she begin to passed out.

Chapter 6

George walked as fast as he could between the two sets of rails while carrying Wanda, and with Maxine running alongside. The dog seemed to sense that something was wrong with Wanda.

The next thing that occurred was exactly what George was afraid would occur—a train whistle sounded from a mile in front of them. George quickly moved over to the side of the track. George could see that the train was a multicar troop train. It was traveling fast so it didn't take long to reach them. As the train passed them, the steam engine shook the rail bed as well as the ground on which George was carrying Wanda. He shielded her head and ears from the noise with his head. Cinders from the smoke stack fell on them.

George's blue shirt was doing its job of stopping the flow of blood from Wanda's body. When they reached the Olson house the ambulance was just pulling up. The police were already there. George very carefully set Wanda onto the stretcher the medical people had waiting alongside the ambulance. Two nurses began working on Wanda immediately, even before and as they moved her into the medical vehicle. Maxine, the German shepherd dog jumped into the ambulance and laid down by Wanda, placing her head on her shoulder. They were soon on the way to the Harriet Hospital. Mildred traveled along with her and Maxine.

George felt he had to do something to catch the two rapists. He felt that it was more important to start his search for the culprits rather than attend to Wanda. She was in good hands with nurses and her mother. Exactly how he was to accomplish the task of capturing the perpetrators was a seemingly impossible task but he needed to start immediately. He found Thomas and got his permission to be gone for a few days, if he needed the time. "You may take as long as you need, George," Thomas said, "just be careful. Don't get hurt yourself. Find those culprits as soon as you can."

"What you need to do," George said to his boss, "is to pray that, when I find the two rapist, I won't kill them with my bare hands. I will need to bring them back to stand trial. Thomas, you need to go to the hospital to be with your wife and your daughter. Organize the church people into a prayer group."

George knew from listening to the hobos traveling in the boxcars that the hobo's best place to hide was in one of the hobo towns. So that is where he would began his search. One of the most famous hobo towns in the United States was the one in Central Wisconsin, just a few miles east from Harriet. George assumed that the two bums were drunk from some cheap booze they had consumed prior to when they committed their sex crime. They would most likely find some more booze and keep drinking. He needed to hurry to the hobo town before they realized and remembered what they had done or passed out in some shack or woods.

After one hour, George entered the Badger hobotown at about 5:30 in the afternoon. The place was crowded with every type of drifter traveling for an assortment of reasons and excuses. His mind was crowded with various thoughts and worries and he had trouble thinking clearly. He once again asked the Lord to help him, this time in the Japanese language:

Chapter 6

主、天のあなたは素晴らしい医師。これらの 2 つの罪人を検索し、正義にそれらをもたらす助けてください。ワンダ、アーメンの癒しを与えます.When he had finished praying he looked up to the skies. He suddenly had an idea.

George had two clues that Wanda had given him. One was that there were two men that committed the sex crime, and the second, one was wearing a red coat. He decided to walk the entire area of the badger hobo town while it was still daylight. Several times he saw two hobos together, but no red coat on just one of them.

Just when he was about to give up, he spotted two men leaning up against a tree, one wearing a red coat, and both of them looking very drunk and very guilty. The probability that he had his guilty men right in front of him was high enough to zero in on these two. "How am I going to bring them in," he said out loud. "I have a plan," he continued talking to himself. "If I can get them into a boxcar going back through Harriet and then cause the train to stop." His mind was going faster than he could record the plan in his mind. He decided to take one step at a time.

"Hey guys, are you interested in staying in a shack where there are three soft beds and plenty of good food? Some booze also. I will share it with you if you team up with me. It's from my rich uncle." George knew it was a sin to tell a lie, but God may permit this little tale.

"Yes, we are interested in teaming up with you," they answered in a slurred speech. They were still very drunk. They were almost unable to stand up.

The three of them were soon on an open boxcar moving toward Harriet. There were a few other people on the same car. Two of them were women. The two culprits looked the women over and probably thought of the good time they had with Wanda. The thought of that made George move to the threshold of attacking them and strangling them with his bare hands. Then he remembered what he told Thomas to pray. George needed to control himself.

The train was like the one that George rode in on when he came to Harriet from California. If everything went right the train would slow down as it approached and entered Harriet. It was dark and the two rapists did not recognize the fact that they were once again entering Harriet. George just hoped that the engines would slow down enough so he could get them off the train without any difficulty.

Soon he saw the sign that said "Harriet one mile." It was time to take action. He knew where the long grass was along the track. He picked up a 3 foot long 2 x 4 and from in back of the two rapists, George hit them both quickly and hard on the heads—one at a time. They were out cold. He then quickly took out the roll of duct tape from his coat pocket and bound their hands and feet. He pulled them to the edge of the boxcar open door and watched for the Olson house, the scrap yard, and the long grass. Quickly he pushed them out of the railcar and into the soft grass and weeds. A few seconds later he jumped out himself, landing in some tall weeds that cushioned his body from the fall. George did not expect to hit the ground as hard as he did. He looked at his legs and saw where he would have some bruises in a few days.

Chapter 6

Four of the church members along with Mildred were still sitting at the Olson kitchen table and praying at 9 p.m. George knocked before entering the kitchen. "George," one of the members spoke in a surprised tone, "you're back already."

"Someone quickly call the sheriff and tell him to get over here with two sets of handcuffs and two sets of leg cuffs."

Soon the two rapists were in the city jail. George then went directly to the hospital to see Wanda. Her mind and body was in shock and she apparently was unable to talk clearly. George just looked at her through the glass window and then decided to go home. He thought that she may confuse him with one of the rapist since he was the first person she had seen after the crime. One of the doctors thought it may be a good idea, also.

Wanda was in the hospital for the next week. She required 3 surgeries and lots of rest. When she did come home, Mildred moved her sleeping quarters to the downstairs guest room. George saw her only briefly from the kitchen when the guest bedroom door was open. According to Mildred she never asked about George. He attributed this to her being ashamed.

Mildred took her daughter to the doctor every other day to make sure her body was healing properly. The doctor was not sure if Wanda would be able to bear children because of her injuries.

One Tuesday when Wanda went alone to see the doctor, he asked her how she was feeling. "I have been feeling a little sick, but only in the morning. Maybe my stomach is a little upset from eating strange food." The doctor took notice of what she had just said.

"How often has this happened?" The good doctor asked. Wanda knew where this questioning was going. She hung her head and softly answered, "at least once every morning for the last 4 days."

"Well, you need to have a pregnancy test. The unthinkable may have happened," the doctor remarked. Wanda suddenly rested her face in her hands.

"I was afraid of that," she responded. The doctor wrote out a lab test order.

"Take this down the hall and give it to the nurse at the desk. We should have the results in a day or so." Wanda took the piece of paper from the doctor and just looked at it for 10 seconds.

"Doctor, tell me what are my options? Is an abortion one of them?" The doctor looked at Wanda for a short time with a look that showed that he was expecting this question.

"Wanda, an abortion would be the last option on my suggested list to your predicament. Let me give you the complete list of suggested options. First, and these are not in any order of preference, find a loving couple to give the little baby to. Second, find a nice young man who would make a fine husband and a good dad, marry him, and have him adopt the baby. Next, give the baby to your parents and let them raise the little tyke. Finally, do not even think about placing an abortion on the list. I am sure that your mom and dad would never go for an abortion."

"Thank you doctor, I need to go. See you tomorrow."

The next afternoon, as they were about to leave for home, the nurse came up to Mildred and spoke. "The doctor wishes to speak with you alone." Mildred wondered what he wanted.

Maybe he wants to talk about the bill that Wanda has run up, she thought to herself. The nurse led her into an empty room and asked

Chapter 6

her to wait a short time for the doctor. Wanda went to the car and waited. She knew what the subject of the conversation between her mother and the doctor would be.

The doctor soon walked in and sat down in a chair next to Mildred. He opened a folder with Wanda's name and looked at Mrs. Olson. "What I am about to tell you may be good news or bad news, Mrs. Olson. Your daughter is pregnant." The room was suddenly quiet for a few seconds. A train on the tracks 6 blocks away was the only sound that Mildred and the doctor could hear.

"I was halfway expecting this news. Does Wanda know this?" She asked the doctor.

"Wanda and I discussed it just yesterday," the doctor answered. "She knew it before she took the test. I must tell you she asked about getting an abortion."

"Her father and I are surely against that," Mrs. Olson responded.

"I must tell you that Wanda may wish to make her own decision," the doctor responded to her comment. "Based on how she got pregnant, you may consider letting her have some input in the decision."

"A procedure like an abortion would need her parent's signature, am I correct doctor?" Mildred questioned.

"You are so correct, Mrs. Olson, and we doctors and this hospital would never approve of it or perform it."

Both parents agreed that they would attempt to talk Wanda out of an abortion, both on religious and cultural grounds. She was not in the kitchen when they were discussing the subject.

George had not said anything to Wanda after finding her in the gully and carrying her injured body back to the house. He asked Mildred to tell Wanda that he wanted to talk to her. She had been ignoring her girlfriends, the boys from her high school senior class, and her college friends, because they all would be asking her embarrassing questions. She felt ashamed and sickened about the whole affair. The newspaper reported that the crime was still under investigation. No names were given as to the victim, the accused persons, George's involvement, or the location. This got all the people in Harriet talking, guessing, and gossiping.

Thomas and Mildred had a church meeting on a Tuesday evening. Mildred spoke to Wanda before they left. "Wanda, now would be a good time to talk to George and thank him for rescuing you from that gully—after all, you could have bled to death. All you need to do is to thank him."

"I know that mother," she responded with remorse in her voice, "but I know what he is going to tell me if I tell him that I am thinking of having an abortion."

"What is he going to tell you, Wanda?" Mildred asked.

"He is going to tell me not to get an abortion."

"We are telling you that, Wanda," her mother answered. "So what is the difference if he tells you also?"

"It's just that I have mixed feelings about him. He is such a kind and considerate person, and he will talk in a convincing manner. I may even agree with him. But I have my future to think of. I want to continue my schooling and become a nurse."

Chapter 6

"Just keep in mind, Wanda," Mildred said, "that no way are we going sign a release form for you to have an abortion."

That evening Wanda was home alone with George. She was in her bedroom and he was in the living room. They both had in their minds the idea to speak with each other, but were not sure how to begin the conversation. Wanda viewed George as a person who had great wisdom for his age. Finally, Wanda walked to the kitchen and started to make some hot chocolate for the two of them. She walked to the door of the living room. "George, I am making some hot chocolate for you and I. Ok?"

"Sounds like a winner, Wanda. Three Large marshmallows please."

"You have it," she answered. This broke the ice between them. Soon Wanda walked into the living room with two cups of steaming hot chocolate with marshmallows protruding out of the rim of the large cups. She set one of them down on the coffee table in front of where George was sitting on one end of the couch and the other on the same table in front of where she sat down on the opposite end of the couch.

"Thank you Wanda," he said. "It is so kind of you."

"Actually George, I owe you 10,000 cups of hot chocolate for saving my life in that pit or gully or whatever you call it. I never want to see it ever again." Wanda was quiet for a moment as she was about to lose her composure and start up crying once again. George had heard her weeping soon after she came home from the hospital and at various times at night. "I want to thank you for rescuing me."

"Wanda, you have been through a terrible ordeal for the past few weeks. I just wish I could have protected you so it would not have happened. But now, let me ask you what are your plans with the little beautiful life growing inside of you?"

"So, you know about that too," Wanda said.

"Yes I do," admitted George. "Mildred told me."

"Well, after doing some extensive thinking, I have halfway decided to get an abortion out in California," she said in a slow and almost guilty voice. George had heard this news also from Thomas one day while working in the scrap yard. He needed to somehow convince Wanda that to do so would be a terrible mistake. In responding to her he decided to play dumb.

"Tell me, Wanda, exactly what an abortion is? I'm not very smart and knowledgeable," George asked in an ignorant manner. "Is that the same as an adoption?" Wanda couldn't believe her ears in listening to George's ignorance. However, she suddenly realized that he was brought up in a different culture where his parents or friends at school possibly never talked about such things. Wanda also sensed that he was playing dumb on purpose. "I am not too well versed with some English words."

"George, I hate to tell you this, but an abortion is, and I am going to be very blunt, where the doctor or a medical technician kills the baby inside the mother. Then he takes the baby out of the mother, sometimes piece by piece. Many hospitals will not perform this procedure. But there are some back alley places that will—for a large fee." George sat for the next full minute while looking at Wanda and taking occasional sips of his hot chocolate and eating marshmallows. His reaction to what she had just told him would go a long way in convincing her to not have the abortion. He knew that Wanda viewed

Chapter 6

his knowledge of certain things as being limited—abortion was one of them. "Do you understand what I just told you, George?"

"I think I do, but probably not if I heard you correctly. Or, maybe I don't want to believe you." George shifted his body on the sofa and sat up. "Wanda, what you are telling me is murder. That is against God's law."

"But what those two men did to me was against God's law also," Wanda retorted.

"Wanda, for God's sake, please don't do this, I beg you. That little life inside of you is a soul that God has placed into your care, even though it was not of your will and it was done in a cruel manner. I will help you raise that little one." Wanda suddenly stood up and left the room and went upstairs to her own room. She wasn't sure what George meant by his last statement. She was left to guess.

"Did he mean that he would offer to marry me in order to save the life of my baby? I would rather give the baby away to some stranger. That way I could finish my nursing education and get a job in a hospital. If I wanted to get married, Bruce or one of my other friends would marry me rather than George. And I would rather marry Bruce—or maybe a doctor.

The rape trial began as quickly as possible since Harriet did not have adequate jail space and it was full already. The jail had 6 cells and they were occupied by individuals waiting for trial or serving time. Two of those cells needed to be emptied. A portable jail was brought in. Wanda and George were the witnesses for the prosecution. Wanda and George met with a lawyer two days prior to the opening session. The defense attorney was able to convince the two rapists to plead guilty and obtain a reduced sentence of 10 years instead of 20 years in the state penitentiary. The two admitted that they were both alcoholics with no hope of recovery unless they were admitted to an institution where that behavior was monitored by force for a long period of time. The trial lasted only three days, including the sentencing.

The next day one of the farmers from rural Harriet drove in with a load of scrap farm machinery. The farmer drove onto the scale and George recorded the gross weight. The customer then drove down a dirt road where George told him to drive and started to unload the trailer. George then disappeared into the metals room and began to sort nonferrous metal and surplus contributions.

The farmer was a new customer and had looked slightly suspicious to George. He thought he had better keep his eye on the middle aged farmer. He went outside and observed the area where the customer was unloading the farm machinery. As he was watching, the farmer suddenly pushed a good size rock off the back of his trailer. Then he grabbed a hold of a rock twice the size of the first rock and pushed it off. "This guy needs to be taught a lesson." George said out loud. He guessed that the two rocks weighed a total of 500 pounds.

The farmer soon appeared back at the scale and was expecting George to weigh his car and trailer to determine the tare for the transaction. The farmer was very surprised when George motioned for the farmer to follow him back to the place where he unloaded the scrap. George then motioned for the farmer to back up directly to the big heavy rocks. The farmer exited his car and had a puzzled look on his face wondering what the worker of the Olson Scrap Metal was up to.

"Ok sir, we need to lift these two rocks back onto your trailer. You will need to take them home again with you. There are two reasons you need to do this. Number 1, you were about to do something that is

Chapter 6

very dishonest. Number 2, you have some children in your car. What are you teaching them? You need to be an example to them. OK?"

"You are correct. I am so sorry," the farmer said.

George did not talk to Wanda for the next couple of weeks. They would see each other around the house, as they passed each other, and at the meal table. He wondered if she was really serious about her proposed action concerning her baby. He never heard Thomas or Wanda talking about this subject either. *I think that her parents are hoping that somehow she changes her mind*, he thought.

Two weeks after the trial had been completed, Wanda walked down to the breakfast table wearing a new maternity dress. George saw her as she stepped on the top step of the stairs. He then looked away and did not look at her again until she sat down at the breakfast table. George recognized that the material that Mildred had used on the dress was from a flour sack.

"Mildred," George said, "You did a good job on that dress." Everyone was quiet.

"Thank you for the complement, George," Mildred said. "The toast that we are eating this morning was made with the flour in that sack." When Wanda was done with eating breakfast, she excused herself from the table and left the house to see one of her friends—probably Jill Miller. George thought it would be a good time to talk to his host parents about Wanda.

"Mildred and Thomas, may I talk to you freely about your daughter?" George said with a serious look.

"George," Thomas spoke directly, "You are part of our family, so tell us whatever is on you mind."

"Yes, please do," Mildred added. George had their undivided attention.

"The story of Wanda could end up badly, unless we acquire a mountain of prayer. I feel the forces of evil have been unleashed against her and we need to fortify the forces of heaven to counteract this evil" George stopped at that point and waited for Mildred or Thomas' response. They were very quiet—just sat still. Finally, George spoke again. "I have told her my opinion of her getting an abortion. I also told her I would help her raise her baby if she would not have an abortion and have the baby and keep it."

"Just what did you mean by that statement, George?" Mildred asked.

"Wanda had the same question and expression on her mind, also, when we stopped our talk. I will let you guess what I meant. We'll need to see how the next chapter of her story goes."

Since the trial for the two tramps was now over, for the next 2 days Wanda prepared to leave Harriet and go to California to have an abortion. She never let on that she was preparing to leave. How long would she be gone? Mildred guessed for at least a full month counting the time it would take for her to heal up. Wanda had saved up money she earned at odd jobs since in the 6th grade.

Wanda was becoming increasingly bitter about her predicament. It was becoming difficult for her to remain pleasant to her parents

Chapter 6

and friends in Harriet. Even George was noticing that Wanda was becoming more hostile in her conversation and interaction with people. She had stopped attending church where she had been teaching Sunday school. She was starting to blame God for permitting this horrible thing to happen to her. Having been raped by a tramp was bad enough, having been raped by two tramps was much worse, and having to have become pregnant by one of them was unbearable. As she was sitting in the apple grove and thinking about herself, she asked God, "Why have you let this happen to me? I don't understand. Please reveal the purpose and reason to me at some point."

George began to suspect that Wanda was planning to run away from home and go to California to seek out an abortion on her own. He never let the Olsons know his suspicions. He kept them only to himself.

One thing that he did do was to slip the address of the internment camp in Stockton, California where his family was, into her suitcase when he saw it open on her bed. He also slipped in $200 in cash along with a note. The note read: 'Wanda—do not use any of this money for an abortion.' He would never tell Mildred and Thomas about this.

Chapter 7

Wanda did promise George that if and when she would go to California, she would try to find where his family was being interned and go visit them. He had heard from them only the one time since he left them on that Sunday afternoon in 1942. He had been reluctant to make more than the one contact with them lest the authorities come and get him and intern him also. He gave Wanda some of his savings to use for travel to their place of residence in Stockton, California. He had read in the newspapers that one of the internment camps for the Japanese people was just on the outskirts of that city. They may have moved them, however.

George thought that the Olsons might think that he may be encouraging Wanda to have the abortion by giving her money. However, he was using this divergent plan to get her mind off the abortion idea. He knew his parents, when they met Wanda, would try talk her out of having one, once they found out she was with child. He knew that his parents would react in the same manner as her parents.

Wanda's parents, Thomas and Mildred Olson, along with their entire church were praying that she would change her mind and not have an abortion. Many in the town of Harriet understood the pain and mental strain that she had suffered, from something that was

Chapter 7

not her fault. To know that the result of this trauma was inside her, was much more than most people would be able to bear. Many of them thought it was justified for Wanda to have an abortion—many did not. The news of what had happened and what may be about to happen was now known by the town through the gossip mill in a short period of time.

The subject of abortion was a mostly unknown word in the small town of Harriet. The word abortion was almost as unsaid as the word pregnant in the classrooms. The school teachers were not allowed to date or get married while teaching during the year. It wasn't known who policed these rules or how many times the rules had been broken.

It had been an unusually busy fall and winter for the Olson Scrap Iron and Metal Company. The collected scrap farm machinery brought in was almost more than George could handle. He decided to put in 60 hours a week to keep up. He even worked through rain and snow to prepare the steel for shipping. His time was too valuable for him to spend on loading the cut up steel on the railcars. He needed to be spending his time on the cutting torch. Thomas hired a few of the tramps from the railroad tracks to get the loading of cars done. Thomas kept his eagle eyes on them for any shenanigans, like boozing on the job.

The railroad had made a deal with Thomas whereby they would keep gondola cars available at all times, if he would guarantee that nothing would be shipped by truck. The railroad would also provide the best freight price. Because of the war, railroad cars were in short supply, especially the flat bed cars. They were needed for shipping the army trucks, jeeps, tanks and large construction equipment. The Harriet area Roadmaster did the best he could to keep the rail cars available for Thomas' business. Both the road master and Thomas spent weekends fishing and sometimes hunting together.

One morning Wanda turned up missing at the Olson breakfast table. There was not a huge amount of excitement or shock when it was discovered. They were all expecting it to take place. The first to say anything was George. "I would suggest that you see if she is upstairs and then see if her bank account has been drained. If it is, then we know where she has gone."

"Maybe we should have aided her more in this stage of her situation," Thomas added. "At this point I think prayer is the only thing that will help. At least it will keep her safe."

"Let me check her room," Mildred said as she stood up. "Let me see what is missing, see what medicines she maybe took with her, and if she left a note."

Mildred went upstairs and looked around Wanda's room for a few minutes. She came downstairs and announced that "nothing is missing except her suitcase, her bag of toiletries, some of her clothes, and the medicines she got from Doc Thysell." George looked at both Mildred and Thomas and could tell that they were very gloomy and needed cheering up.

"Let me offer a short prayer to brighten this gloomy time for the mom and dad."

> *Lord, Wanda's parents have done a good job of raising their daughter. You have sent me to them for a purpose and that purpose is as yet only partially completed. I know that all is going to come out well.*

Chapter 7

Give Mom and Dad hope and good cheer as they go through this day. Send two guardian angels down to protect Wanda.—Amen.

On her way to California by bus, Wanda had much time to think. A worry that dominated some of her thinking time was how she would be rejected by her friends in Harriet and at her college. What boys would want her now? "Bruce is my only hope," she said out loud. She had not even talked to him since the criminal act against her was committed. She knew that George was interested in her, but that is where the interest stopped. Her upbringing by her parents and church had ingrained in her that mixing the races was wrong. She had never thought about why she believed it or if there was any biblical basis for it. At this point she even thought about giving up on marriage—but maybe not.

George had warned her once again before she left on the bus about the strange and tricky men she may run into on the bus and in any city. "Stay clear of them," he said, "watch where you walk, don't walk down alleys, and find a policeman if you get lost. Expect guardian angels to be by your side. One more thing, sit on the bus where the bus driver can see you and where you can see the bus driver."

Wanda's next thought was about the fortunate circumstances of George landing on the family yard that July morning in 1942. Although she wouldn't admit it to anyone, George was the best thing that happened to her family. *I don't know what my dad would have done if it were not for the help of George starting in the summer of 1942,* she thought. *All of the good young workers went off to one of two wars.*

Wanda was tired but wasn't able to get much sleep on the bus. She would drift off into dreams that were more nightmares than pleasant visions. The one recurring image she had was being attacked and thrown down into the trench next to the railroad track. Her back and legs were still aching from hitting her bare legs and back on the gravel, stones, and tree roots at the bottom.

Next, she couldn't seem to get her mind off George. A feeling of guilt was beginning to creep into her mind. The relationship she displayed with him was not what she was capable of. She knew and felt, ever since he showed up on the Olson lawn, that George liked her and wished to have a romantic relationship with her. His personality and kindness she attributed to his relationship to his Lord and his upbringing. It was the reason that her parents took him in and showed kindness to him right from the beginning. "I never showed much heartfelt kindness to him," she said to herself. "When and if I see him again, I need to maybe reverse that feeling and behavior."

Back in Harriet a group of the people in the church were meeting in prayer for Wanda every week. The group was organized by Mildred. Some of the group were praying daily. George prayed as he was working in the scrap yard and in the fur house. (With his eyes open, of course.)

He prayed privately out of respect for the relationship between Wanda and her friend Bruce. He may be an answer to Wanda's need for a husband and a dad for her baby, if and when she may decide to go that route. George wasn't up to date how exactly that relationship was going or how it would turn out. Wanda's friend Jill Miller

Chapter 7

had told George that their relationship had grown cold. Her parents, Thomas and Mildred were not in favor of her relationship since Bruce was not a Christian. Bruce even admitted it.

George received a letter from Jill Miller one afternoon in the daily mail. It was an invitation to a party at church on the following Saturday afternoon and evening. It was a church function where the girls would invite the boys. George wrote on the card that he would accept. Instead of mailing the card back to Jill, he walked 5 blocks to Jill's home and handed the card to her. "Hi Jill, I thought I would save a 3 cent stamp and walk my reply to you. It's a positive reply."

"That's great, George," she answered. "I was hoping that you would be able to come. I need to tell you something about my invite to you." George begin wondering what thing Jill was about to add.

"Go ahead Jill."

"I know that you have had a thing for Wanda since you came to Harriet, also that Wanda has told me more than once that she for some reason does not care for you even though you probably saved her life. I do not wish to barge in on what either of you think is your territory, but I like you and I think you are too nice of a guy to keep you all cooped up in a scrap yard. I will tell Wanda when she comes back from California." George thought for a moment then replied.

"Thank you Jill for that vote of confidence."

Wanda arrived at the bus depot in Stockton, California and found Mac's Diner only a block away. She ordered the Special hamburger, French fries, and an O' So Grape soda pop. The waitress was very nice and friendly. "Miss, can you tell me where I can find the Japanese internment camp?" she asked the waitress. "I think it's somewhere outside the city of Stockton."

"You don't look Japanese," the waitress responded with a questionable look on her face.

"I need to look up a family for a friend of mine," Wanda replied.

"You are not very far from it. Just take the green bus that comes on this corner. It runs every hour. It will take you within a few blocks of the camp." The waitress walked to another booth to wait on another customer. Wanda soon got her meal and Grape soda pop. As the waitress was about to leave the table once again, Wanda spoke to her once more.

"Miss, I have another question for you, and you may not know the answer."

"Ask me and I will try to help you," the waitress answered back. Wanda was a little hesitant to ask what was on her mind. She cupped her mouth to indicate that she didn't want people to hear her.

"Do you know of any place where a girl could get an abortion?" Wanda asked. The waitress suddenly had a very surprised look on her face.

"You?!" the waitress replied as she pointed to Wanda. "Let me sit down by you. I am set to go on a break shortly. My name is Julie. Start from the beginning. I have a half hour."

"I am Wanda. Yes, me," Wanda answered. "I'm from Wisconsin and a few weeks ago I was raped along the railroad tracks. Apparently my insides were not too badly hurt and last week the doctor told me

Chapter 7

that I was with child. I just don't care to have a child from either of those two creeps."

"Oh, there were two guys involved," Julie replied. "Is that correct?"

"Unfortunately, yes," Wanda replied.

"Well, Wanda, let me tell you what happened to me, and I hope that I can influence you to not have one. I was in a similar situation about 3 years ago. I too was in the market for an abortion after a one night stand with a military guy. I didn't even know his name. He shipped out the next morning. He may even be dead by now — killed in action and now is buried in the ground. My parents wanted me to get the abortion, because of all of the social disgrace they would have had heaped upon them. They sent me out here from Oklahoma where we lived. This doctor in this house about a mile from here did the work, which I viewed as butchery. Now, I will never be able to have children, from what the good doctors tell me. Please, don't do this." Julie got up to continue her break somewhere else, probably in the smoking room.

Wanda sat drinking two cups of coffee that she got free, wondering whether or not to believe what she had just heard from Julie. She sounded very truthful and sincere. *Maybe I need to rethink more about this*, she thought to herself. 30 minutes later Wanda was still at the café. She had nowhere else to go and she did not want to roam in a city she did not know, per George's advice. Her thoughts suddenly went back to George's advice she did not regard, about walking along the railroad track in Harriett. *If I had only been more careful how I had dressed, or had just walked in one of the parks in* Harriet.

The waitress Julie came back to her table once again. "I am off duty as of 5 minutes from now. I will be going to my other job where I will be working until midnight. Then its home to bed. I have tomorrow off if you need company. Here is my phone number in case you need any help or have any questions.

"I do have one more question for you Julie," Wanda said.

"Sure, Wanda," Julie responded. "Ask away."

"Tomorrow is Sunday and I am usually found in church. Do you have any churches you could recommend?" Wanda was totally unfamiliar with any churches in California, although she assumed that even California had some Bible preaching churches.

"Well," Julie said, "what brand of church do you like? Catholic, Lutheran, Presbyterian, Baptist, or what?"

"Some church that preaches the gospel, sings the old hymns, serves good coffee afterwards, etc.–the whole nine yards."

"About 3 blocks from here there is a church that has in its membership several ethnic peoples who all speak English," Julie answered. "Just a few months ago they pulled out the Japanese and sent them to an internment camp. All the ethnic peoples thought it was just terrible—all wrong. They would welcome you, I'm sure."

"Thank you Julie," Wanda said, "I will check it out."

Back in Harriet, George and Jill not only went to the Fall Church Youth Festival together, but George invited Jill to the "Surplus Scrap for Victory" Banquet on the following Saturday evening at the City Auditorium in Harriet. All three principals of the Olson Scrap Iron and Metal Company were honored. Jill sat with George at the honored guest table. Almost everyone at the dinner wanted to meet George since they had heard so much about him. Many of the attendees had no idea that they had shaken hands with a half Japanese young man.

Chapter 7

Jill and George became an item in church every Sunday. He helped Jill with her junior high Sunday school class. They ate the Sunday noon meal either at the Olsons or at the Millers. This went on all the while Wanda was out west.

George was busy with preparing steel for shipping in gondola railroad cars. Most of the farm machinery was hauled in on trucks, hay racks, or pulled by horses. In the typical gondola car the maximum amount of 75,000 to 125,000 pounds of prepared steel could be loaded, depending on how well the steel fit together within the car. With tin (sheet metal) it was different, since the Olson Scrap Company did not have a tin baler. Any steel that was 7 Gauge or greater would pass as tin. Any steel below 7 Gauge would go as steel. Tin would include car body tin, steel drums, steel wire, and a host of other pieces of tin found in a scrap yard. Care needed to be taken so that the tin did not become so corroded that only the corrosion remained. Such was the case with tin that was buried in the ground for years—as in during the 1930s.

Automobiles were George's specialty in scrapping. The American auto companies stopped producing very soon after Pearl Harbor and switched over to producing tanks, jeeps, guns, and other war equipment. Both Thomas and George early on saw the need for auto parts to be salvaged and stored for sale since very few companies were able to produce even the parts to repair broken down autos.

After the autos were stripped of its salvageable parts. George would torch off the frame, remove the doors, place them inside the car, and burn it. A 16 ton dozer would then be rented and be used to crush each auto and stacked into an open gondola car.

One of the difficulties in loading the railroad cars was moving them down the track when a segment of the car has been filled up. A rail jack was then used to move the car inch by inch. Care had to be taken when moving the railcar. The rails are normally built on an incline, sometimes making it difficult to control the speed at which the car would move. Occasionally a car will get away from the operator and could crash into a vehicle or anything crossing the track at intersections. The reason for the incline was so that the local freight train could drop off the railcar(s) and (they) would move freely to where it could be stopped by the handbrake on top of the car.

The Olsons kept wondering what they should do about looking for their missing daughter. Should they put out an APB bulletin by the police, wait for Wanda to show up back in Harriet, or send George after her? They were over a barrel. If they publicized the missing person, it may attract the authorities and shed light on George. They would then take a chance of having the internment police snag George. Then they would have two of their family missing. They decided to pray and wait.

Another reason the Olsons were hesitant to publicize the Wanda missing person situation was that it may create a huge national story that involved a Japanese-American. It would get wide publicity. The Olsons did want not that.

Chapter 7

It would not be long before the business would be into the raccoon and other fur season. The number of the furry creatures this year was more than any other year that the old time trappers could remember. Probably the reason was because it had been 15 years since there had been a season on them. The average price for raccoon this year was going to be, as thought by Thomas, $2 each. In a few months the price could go up significantly.

George and Thomas would be buying them almost as fast as they could process them. They would need to hire students from the Harriet high school to work after school and on Saturdays. It would take about two weeks to complete the job of going from the dead raccoon to the dried skin. Most of that time was in drying the skin. The company in Brooklyn would be making the skins into pilot's vests and helmets as fast as they were able. The company said that they were the best and largest raccoon in the United States. This was because of the water in the lakes, the cold weather, and the corn and other feed that the raccoon ate.

Because of the amount of cash needed to pay the trappers and hunters, Thomas had made an agreement with the fur manufacture in Brooklyn whereby payment would be made within 10 days of the receipt of the shipment of the raccoon skins. The State Bank of Harriet's Board of Directors had voted to punish the scrap business for selling scrap to Japan back in the 1930s by not making any business loans to them. This practice soon backfired on the bank when it became common knowledge within the farming community. Farmers remembered when the business found a market for their scrap in the years during the depression when their families were going hungry. A bank in a neighboring town decided to reward the business by loaning the Olson Scrap and Metal Company money as they needed it.

The other revenue from the raccoon came from the thick layer of fat off the skin when it was taken off with a drawknife on a log. The barrels of fat were used to make glycerin for explosives for the army. Also, the remains of the raccoon were boiled so that it would yield its remaining fat content. What remained was sold to the hog producers, some of it used for fertilizer. An average size raccoon would yield a gallon of fat.

Wanda finished her coffee at the café in Stockton and decided to find a hotel room to get some rest before she looked for and found a facility that provided abortions. She also needed to find George's family at the internment camp as she had promised. She found a small motel that wasn't very expensive. This motel had a small coffee pot and a hotplate for the guests to use along with a variety of coffees. As soon as she had checked in, she laid down and fell asleep.

She soon began to dream. Her mind was back where she lived in Harriet, Wisconsin and it was a strange one. She was still in high school, was walking to class, was about to take a final test, had not studied for the test, and had not even bought or read the book.

Added to those host of predicaments was the fact her class had already finished the test and was passing her on the school steps. Finally, she could not move any part of her body. She suddenly woke up. "What a horrible nightmare," she exclaimed. "Does this have any meaning?"

Chapter 7

She decided to make a pot of coffee. The weather was very warm and mild where she was at in California so she decided to sit out in the evening sun and watch it set. She began to review the past months of her life and see if she could make any sense of it.

She decided to go all the way back to when George showed up on their lawn. Wanda was not too happy when she came downstairs that first morning and found this strange hobo sitting at their breakfast table. Even worse, having her mother treat him as a member of the family made her angry even though she knew that it was the charitable thing to do. Then, Wanda's mother almost forced her into making up a list of things to get for George like it was the command of God. *I guess maybe it was*, she thought.

Wanda was getting tired and once again begin to sleep. This time she fell asleep until 8 a.m. the next morning. It was time to get ready for church if she was going to find it and make it there on time.

When she found the church she was 10 minutes early for Sunday school. The class that she attended was for young college age of about 8 young people. They were talking about making decisions. The question that the class was zeroing in on was: What should young people be careful about, when making decisions? Everyone had a contributing answer. It came around to Wanda's turn to contribute. She was quiet and did not especially care to speak. Finally, she decided to speak up.

"I have never been here before and I know none of you, so I can speak freely to this class, if you will permit me."

"Speak freely," the class leader spoke out.

"Thank you," Wanda replied. "My name is Wanda Olson and I am from Harriet, Wisconsin. 3 months ago I did not heed the warning of a young man who has a crush on me. He told me not to wear sensual clothes when I walked along the railroad tracks. The reason? Where I live there are many hobos, tramps, and bums that hop trains and walk the tracks. They are constantly looking for cheap booze, merchandise to steal and girls and women to take advantage of." Wanda was a good speaker and she had the 8 young people eating out of the palm of her hand. She continued.

"Two days after my half Japanese and half American friend had warned me about my error in choice of dress, two young men in their 20s spotted me. Next, they grabbed me, taped my mouth shut, pulled me into the long grass by the tracks and both had their way with me. I don't need to explain what I am talking about."

"They then carried me to a ditch and threw me into it. I am sure they were leaving me for dead. Interesting thing, my friend reacted quickly found me and kept me from bleeding to death. He carried me to the medical people and took off to find the criminals at a Hobo town 2 miles away. They are now in jail and going to prison, thanks to his fast acting.

"The bad news is that I am with child from one of those two rapists. That is the reason I am in this community at this time. I am seeking to get an abortion."

"That is the basis for a good love story and I suppose that you will now marry the boy who saved you," a young women said to Wanda.

"Not really, ma am," Wanda responded, "I am thankful for his saving my life, but I don't really love him enough to marry him. That is not a good reason, I guess, that a girl should marry a boy just because he saved her life, or that it would solve a pregnancy situation.

Chapter 7

She needs to be in love with him." Wanda was almost certain that she was hitting home with some of the young people she was addressing.

"However," Wanda said with a change of subject matter, "let me give you something else to chew on." She was now ready to formulate the discussion question for the class.

"The reason I am here in California is because I am looking for an abortion. Two people raped and got me with child. Now what do I do? You, class, need to come up with a decision. Should I get an abortion?" The class all of a sudden became very quiet. It seemed that no one wished to comment. Finally a girl in the back row spoke up.

"Have you asked God what to do?"

CHAPTER 8

After asking certain people, Wanda found a location that would provide abortions to individuals who could pay the healthy fee. It was in a building that was in the middle of the block. The front door to the building was accessed by walking down an alley. She talked to a woman at a desk just inside the front door. The woman covered the entire procedure, which Wanda had a hard time believing. The facility was nothing like what Wanda was used to in a hospital. It was dirty, it smelled, and the personnel were not acting like professionals. She felt depressed when she had finished the tour. She also felt that they were not telling her the complete story. Wanda would need to find a job and work almost full time to pay for it. It was not very satisfying to her, after being involve with helping in actual births back home in the hospital where she was taking her training. She decided to wait a few days before making a final decision on whether to go further.

As she was not well versed on the subject of abortion, her whole situation seemed to be getting darker and darker. She was starting to feel very uneasy about what she was wanting to do. It felt like someone was praying for her. Meanwhile, she thought she would try

Chapter 8

to find George's family. She had the idea that this was one way she could repay him for saving her life.

The address of the internment camp was found in her suitcase that she had on her bed in Harriet. How it got there she could only guess, but she was sure it was George. Found in the same place was an envelope with $100 in 5 dollar bills. He probably figured that there was no better way of spending the money he was making than to use it to assist Wanda in finding his family and getting to meet them.

From the city directory she found where the Japanese internment camp was located and where the government was keeping some of the Japanese people. Just like the waitress at the café told her, there was a city bus that was traveling to the camp and the bus driver gave her a free ride. The bus driver was a woman, probably because of the shortage of available men. "You look like someone from the Midwest. Am I correct?" the bus driver asked.

"You are correct," Wanda responded, "Wisconsin, as a matter of fact."

"So what are you doing out here?"

"I have some business to attend to. I also need to contact a Japanese family at the internment camp," Wanda added.

"I wish this war would get over so these poor people could go back to their homes," the bus driver said empathetically. "Although, the war has given many people jobs that they would have not otherwise obtained."

"Will this bus take me back to the city?" Wanda asked.

"Yes, it runs 24 hours a day."

When the bus arrived at the internment camp office, Wanda was able to secure the building number of where George's family was being held. It was a large building where many families were being held. An 8 foot fence surrounded the camp. Children were outside with their mothers attending them. Playground equipment was being used by many of the children. There were sandlot baseball games in progress.

She walked up to the apartment door with the number that was given to her at the office. She knocked three knocks. A medium size man opened the door very slowly. The man was almost the exact image of George, only George was at least 4 inches taller. "Are you George's dad?" She asked in a relatively loud voice, thinking he may not understand English very well. Suddenly, the entire family, upon overhearing George's name, came quickly into the room and were quiet. "My name is Wanda, I am from Wisconsin."

"Yes, I am George's dad," the man replied in an English that was almost perfect. "My name is Jiro Robinson." He became suspicious thinking that the federal officials may be trying to find George so they could intern him also. Wanda looked at the family and noticed that the mother looked Scandinavian and was very much pregnant. The mother finally walked up to Wanda and took her hand.

"My name is Veronica. How do you know our George?" she asked.

"He took a freight train from California to my parents' home in Wisconsin where he is now working in my father's business." The father seemed to relax a little upon hearing Wanda's words. "He asked me to tell you that the people he is staying with, which is my family, are good Christian people. George misses all of you."

Wanda took George's mother's hand and spoke, "you were a missionary in Japan, weren't you."

Chapter 8

"George told you, didn't he?" she answered.

"Yes he did," Wanda answered, with a quick realization that George was a direct copy of his mom and dad. They were almost like her own parents in their character.

The Father, upon hearing Wanda's words, gathered everyone in a circle, joined hands, and offered a prayer of thanksgiving. George's mother squeezed Wanda's hand and began to weep tears of joy.

"I suppose you wonder why our last name is an American name." Mrs. Robinson asked.

"I am curious," Wanda answered. "George never told us."

"It's a long story. My first name is Veronica. My maiden name was Sandberg. My husband's former life was not very good. He thought he should change his last name after he became a Christian. When we got married, the pastor who performed the wedding ceremony was named Robinson. So I asked him if we could use his name. That's the true story."

The Japanese family's invitation to bed overnight was readily accepted by Wanda. The family freed up a sofa for her to sleep on. Wanda observed the blankets on the sofa and concluded that it must get rather chilly during the evening and nighttime hours. However, Wanda was used to the chilly nights in Wisconsin.

It was only 10 minutes later and the mother asked Wanda two questions. "What kind of tea would you like? And, can I fix you something to eat?" George had warned Wanda that his mother would want to entertain her with food and drink and that it would be unkind to refuse to accept this invitation.

"Yes, please," Wanda responded with a smile.

"What would you like to drink," she asked. Wanda was glad that she asked that question. Normally a host would bring whatever everyone else was drinking, which could be an alcoholic beverage, which Wanda knew that George did not drink. It was the same with Wanda.

"How about coffee or tea?" Wanda replied.

"Actually, I have both. I have made a habit of drinking a Japanese drink—tea, and a Norwegian drink—coffee, in the morning. I have found that the two mix well in the stomach."

"Bravo, I'll take tea," Wanda answered. "For something to eat, I will eat whatever your family is eating."

"How about Corn Flakes and toast?" Veronica asked.

"Bravo, once again," Wanda approved.

During the night the mother cried out with birth contractions. Since no qualified professional was in the area, Wanda took charge and administered care to her, rubbing her back, legs and feet. George's mother soon fell asleep. Then Wanda fell asleep immediately after lying down on the couch.

Wanda had helped with delivering babies at her college hospital and was not hesitant to offer help. "We have no maternity care during the night here at the camp—only during the day," the father said in the morning, "and it is not very good. The military has most of the doctors stationed at other internment camps."

"Well, guess what?" Wanda said, "I don't think that this baby is going to wait, I will stay here and keep my eye on your wife." Wanda was no doctor but knew the signs of the imminent birth in a pregnant mother.

Chapter 8

About 3 in the afternoon, the mother began having severe pains. Then her water suddenly broke. She began having greater contractual pains. The father helped to clean up the mess. The mother suddenly relaxed and began to sleep in between the pains.

When George's mother woke up, one of his sisters brought her mother some food to eat. Wanda had a chance to visit with her. As they were talking, Wanda had to go to the bathroom. When she returned George's mother said to Wanda, "May I ask you a question?"

"You may," she replied.

"You act like you are pregnant." Wanda looked up with a smile. "Are you?" Veronica asked.

"May I tell you my story Mrs. Robinson?" Wanda asked.

"I am a good listener," she answered.

"You may not believe this, but here goes and your son is very much a part of this story. When I came home from college last summer your son gave me a warning thru my mother that I disregarded. As a result I almost lost my life. George advised me not to wear sensual clothes when I walked along the railroad tracks. We live along a major railroad track, where there are many bad men who roam and walk. Well, I walked too many times and one morning two of these men attack me. They tied my hands and covered my mouth with tape. I don't need to tell you what happened next.

"Oh no," George's mother said with concern.

"When they were finished with me they threw me down into a ravine and luckily Maxine the German shepherd dog found me.

George lifted me out. He kept me from bleeding to death and carried me 1 mile back to the house. From there I was taken to the hospital."

"You are ok now, aren't you?" George's mother asked.

"Only that now I am pregnant as a result. And that is what brings me to California. I want an abortion." George's mother covered her face for the next 15 seconds. She finally uncovered her face and stared at Wanda.

"Wanda, may I say something to you?"

"You may," Wanda answered.

"When we sent George on the freight in the summer of 1942, it almost broke my heart. As he was riding away from us that day, The Lord spoke to me and said, *'George is going to be all right. I have a special job for him where he is going.'* If you get an abortion it will not be what God wants."

At that moment, Veronica suddenly begin to have additional birthing pains. "Get me a pan of water so I can wash my hands, and some clean sheets, towels, and clothes." Wanda examined the mother and realized that the baby was about to be born. She asked George's father to help her with the delivery. "I hope that you have done this before," she said to him.

"Actually, I have, when George was bor in Japan," he answered. It was an easy delivery. The same with the other children, although they were both born in a hospital in Los Angeles. You and I should have no problem, if I can remember what to do."

After a painful delivery a baby girl was born. She was no doubt part Japanese and part Swedish. The birth was very difficult for

Chapter 8

the mother. "She better not have any more," Wanda said to the father. "What are you going to name the little girl?" Wanda asked George's father.

"What was your name again?" The mother asked.

"Wanda. W A N D A," she spelled.

"May we use your name?" The mother asked.

"You may," Wanda replied.

"I think I will name my little girl Angelina Wanda," the mother responded.

"Thank you," Wanda replied. "Angelina is a beautiful name."

"So is Wanda," the mother expressed in response.

The mother immediately began to start breastfeeding. Wanda was surprised when the milk came so fast. When she was done and the baby seemed satisfied, Wanda took little Angelina so the mother could get some rest.

Wanda hadn't planned to stay for more than a couple of nights with George's family. However, the Mother's medical condition was still up in the air. She needed more rest and care. Wanda decided to stay since she had not made up her mind about the abortion decision.

Two days later George's father came home with the news that he had talked to the camp administrator about having his wife travel back to Wisconsin with Wanda on the train. The baby was starting to get healthier and Wanda could tend to little Angelina Wanda on the train while the mother rested.

Jiro also wanted his wife to see a doctor in Harriet to make sure that Veronica was well after experiencing a rough pregnancy and delivery. Since he was not working, he would be able to take care of the other children in their family.

George's mother and baby Angelina got ready to leave with Wanda to go back to Harriet, Wisconsin. They decided to take a passenger train to Harriet.

On the way to the train station Wanda made the decision to not pursue the abortion option. She had asked God the question that she was asked by the young girl in the Sunday school class. God's answer was loud and clear.

George's mother was feeding the baby very well since she had plenty of milk. The two women had plenty of time to talk on the train. "I have a question for you, Wanda," Veronica said.

"Asked away, Veronica."

"Does my son have any girl friends in Harriet? He had one in Los Angeles but she was not a Christian like we wanted George's girl to be."

This question was a hard one for Wanda to answer. The expression on her face was very telling to George's mother. She could tell that there was something going on between the two young people. The only answer Wanda could give her was to say nothing. Mrs. Robinson was an expert at discerning a person's feelings. "You have feelings for my son, George, don't you, Wanda?"

"Maybe I do," Wanda answered slowly. "When I first met him, I didn't care for him. I had this hang-up about a mixed race and that is what George is."

"And yet he saved your life from those two rapists," Mrs. Robinson responded.

"I know and I feel terrible about the fact that I have not yet properly thanked George. I guess I just don't know how to thank him. Maybe

Chapter 8

I could ask him finally to take me out—go to a movie or go on a picnic sometime." Wanda knew she should reward George somehow.

"I am going to pray that you will find some way to thank George for saving your life," Veronica said after a long pause.

Wanda sat quiet for the first 100 miles on their way to Harriet—half the time sleeping and half the time thinking—thinking about her possible relationship with George. Weighing the pluses and the minuses of such a union, she finally came to the conclusion that her predicament would best be solved if she and George and her baby could possibly become a family. She could have a built-in baby sitter with Mildred if she wished to start up with college again. It is not what she wished for in the beginning. Going to school and raising a baby at the same time would not be easy.

There was one other important component to this solution that was missing. She and George were not in love—at least she wasn't.

She looked over on the seat next to her and Veronica was sleeping. Her baby was sleeping beside her. They were in the middle of the country and the ride was smooth. Veronica had a very pretty baby. Wanda began wondering if her baby would be cute. Would he or she be healthy? Would he or she be smart? What nationality would the baby be—at least ¼ Swedish and ¼ Norwegian. Would it make any difference what the other half would be? She would probably never know.

Within a few minutes the head of the dining car came in and announced that lunch was being served. This announcement awoke both Veronica and her baby. "Let's go see what there is to eat," Wanda said, "I will buy. I am hungry."

"I need to eat also. My baby is drinking my breast milk like a horse," the mother said. "But that is good."

They were seated at a table and given a menu. "This is the first time I will have eaten on a train," Veronica stated.

It was during this travel to Harriet that Wanda fell in love with the baby Angelina and seemed to forget that she had a little one inside of her. "Maybe I could find a nice couple in Harriet that would want my baby," she said out loud at one point. "It would be the second option on doctor Thysell's list of options."

Back in Harriet the surplus scrap collection business was progressing very well. The price of nonferrous metals had risen substantially. The owners of the Olson Scrap Iron and metal and now Fur Company had profited greatly. They were written up in many newspaper articles and trade journals as to their surplus and scrap organization and the honest business practices they were engaged in.

The Brooklyn Clothing Company that was manufacturing the pilot helmets and vests for the military pilots, were including with each pilot's vest and helmet product a form letter and envelope. The pilot could then send a thank you and comments back to the Olson Fur Company. Thank you replies were received from Alaska, Russia, England, Norway, Sweden, Denmark, France, and several other countries.

The U.S. Government, after Pearl Harbor, asked Americans to salvage and collect a long list of materials that could be used for the war effort. The materials included paper, aluminum, tin, iron and

Chapter 8

steel, rubber, silk stockings, and cooking fat. Sone of these materials, like rubber and silk were scarce because the Japanese had cut off the supply by their rapid advance through Southeast Asia. America got caught with their pants down.

The government organized a major conservation and recycling effort. Cities and states were given quotas. Children and their families were involved with conservation and recycling of goods. Two children in Harriet went down the street with their wagons collecting surplus items of scrap iron, old clothes, scrap paper and cans of fat from the kitchens. They brought the wagons full to a central location for later pickup by truck. The building they brought them to was donated by a widow who wished to participate in the surplus collection, but could not physically help with the pickups.

Given the need for aluminum for aircraft production, drives were launched for old aluminum pots and pans. As the Japanese cut off America from sources of rubber, drives were launched for old tires, inner tubes, rubber bathing caps—anything rubber.

Word got around that many of the children's toys were made of metal. When the Harriet children realized this fact, they began collecting toy tractors, toy farm machinery, train sets, and erector sets for the scrap drive. The children needed something to replace these toys and leave it to kids to think up a replacement toy. There was the rubber guns that used two pieces of rubber from an inner tube along with a piece of ¾ inch x 3" x 36" wood carved into a rifle, and a spring clothespin. A benefit of using this non-threatening toy was that no injury could be inflicted. Contests were being held in various towns and cities between groups of boys and girls.

Because the scrap yard was near the country, there existed the problem of various rodents running around, eating food, multiplying, spreading disease, and raising havoc with the neighbors. Several of the neighbors complained to the city about the Olson Scrap Metal Company spreading the rodent population. It presented a public relation problem to Thomas and George and their business. George came up with a possible solution—Cats and Buckets.

An ad was placed in the Harriet News for any cat that was female and a good mouser. If the cat was about to have kittens, it would be all the better. The cats were provided with a bed of straw and running water. They would be spread out in various places in the scrap yard where there was evidence of rodents of any kind, but given no food. The cats would need to catch their own mice and rats for food. They would roam over to the neighbor's property to catch rodents there also. It was very soon that the neighbors began to notice the decrease in the rat and mouse population.

The buckets were used to drown the rats and mice. A bucket of water was placed where the rats were multiplying. A cup of fat was melted over the top surface of the water and allowed to harden. When the rodent smelled the fat or suet, they would jump into the bucket and drown—good bye mousey.

George and Mildred were reading in the National Surplus, Rations, and Conservation Digest where many communities were starting victory gardens. Many of them were very successful growing massive amounts of vegetables for their communities. "Why can't we do it too," Mildred asked George.

Chapter 8

"We can," George answered. "And I know a good place to start."

"Where?" Asked Mildred. "Where do we have a plot of land that has exceptional soil?"

"On the north end of our property," George responded. "I have tested it out with the cucumbers and onions that I grew for you last spring." Mildred suddenly looked at George.

"Is that where you got them," Mildred asked. "I was wondering. You failed to tell us."

"Let's plan on planting a big garden there next spring. We can open a vegetable stand and use the money for some mission work, or maybe a short vacation. Or, maybe we can just eat them or give the veggies to the needy.

Maxine, the German shepherd dog apparently remembered and was missing Wanda. She slept upstairs in Wanda's bedroom. One of Wanda's wool scarfs was hanging in the corner of the room and there is where Maxine laid on the floor. Whenever the car that Wanda drove to college was driven into the yard by another member of the family, the German shepherd would make a quiet dog crying sound and scurry down the stairs to the front door. She would sit there until she was sure that Wanda was not coming in, which could be for 30 minutes. Then she would walk to the kitchen where Wanda's chair was and would sit underneath it for another 30 minutes, before returning back upstairs to her bedroom.

One other surplus collectible that the government encouraged the public to collect and donate that could be used for defense was in the category of jewelry. This included coins, gold, silver, pewter, watches, rings—any item that had a valuable metal contained therein. These could be used in instrumentation and coatings on military equipment. As the Olson Company collected them, Mildred would bring them to a safety deposit box at the bank. Most of the items were donated for the war effort and not done with any exchange of money.

There were five situations where farmers gave up gold and silver contained in capped sewer pipes that were dug up from the ground. These were buried when the gold standard went out during the depression. Many family members of ex-farmers who had lost their farms due to the depression began to wonder if their family had buried precious metals and jewelry in their fields. Some of the farmers during the early 1930s buried their gold, silver, and diamonds and did not tell any member of their family or draw a map of where they buried them. The old farmer died and the gold and silver was lost forever. A magazine article made reference to this happening whereby some people tried using metol detectors to locate the riches. There were five people in the United States who did find capped sewer pipes with various treasures in them.

The well-meaning city council of Harriet made a serious error with some antiques they had collected during the early 1900s. A new park had been built in celebration with the new century, 1900. Picnic tables were set up, a bandstand was erected, and a civil war memorial was built in memory of names of a few civil war solders from a wide area around Harriet, Wisconsin.

The city fathers thought it would be neat If they could buy some relics of the civil and the revolutionary wars, if they could be located.

Chapter 8

Money was donated for this fund, inquiries were made, and two flatbed railcars of war equipment were shipped from the east and south to Harriet.

Fast forward to 1942, the president called for surplus scrap iron to be collected for the war effort in Japan and in Europe. The city council, without much forethought quickly gathered a railroad car full of the park war antiques and shipped it to Duluth for scrap. The entire city council lost their jobs in the next election.

CHAPTER 9

Wanda, Veronica, and new little baby Angelina were in Harriet within two days after they left the internment camp. The train they were on was a fast moving troop train. During the last 100 miles of the trip, there were many soldiers and sailors on the train. Many of them were good looking and immediately had their eyes on Wanda. However, by this time she had had her life filled with strange men and paid no attention to them. She had nothing to fear in this situation since she not only looked pregnant but was very much pregnant. In addition she was holding a new born baby.

Wanda and Veronica got off at the Harriet train passenger depot and got a ride from the agent to the Olson home. They wanted to surprise Thomas and Mildred. Maxine, the German shepherd dog sensed Wanda was outside in front of the house and began making her 'Wanda is home' whimpering sound—they had missed each other.

Both Thomas and Mildred were very surprised when they walked through the front door on a Sunday afternoon.

"Wanda, you're back," both of Wanda's parents said at about the same time. They gave each other hugs.

Chapter 9

"And who do you have with you?" Mildred asked. She knew who the two guests were as Wanda had called her mother 3 days before from the internment camp.

"Mom and Dad, I want you to meet George's mother, Veronica, and his new baby sister, Angelina Wanda. Yes, I'm back and the first thing I want you to do is to look at my stomach." Mr. and Mrs. Olson looked at their daughter's face and then at her stomach.

"So, did you go through with the abortion?" Mr. Olson asked.

"No, I did not," Wanda said. "Can't you see that?"

"What happened, Wanda?" Mildred asked with a note of surprise, confusion, and happiness.

"I never had an abortion," Wanda replied.

"We are glad. What changed your mind?" Mildred asked.

"George's mother and this little girl," Wanda answered. "His mom was very much pregnant when I arrived at their home. I actually helped deliver her baby. Isn't she cute? I found where the family was living. She had this baby soon after I arrived. They asked me to help with the delivery after they found out that I was studying nursing and had worked in a delivery room. They have very poor maternity services out there in the camps. They are short of doctors because of the war. George has a new little baby sister. Where is George? It was a hard delivery because of the age of George's mother. We almost lost her."

"He is out in the scrap yard." Mildred replied. "I know you wish to talk to him. He will be glad to see you and his mother."

"I'm sorry that I didn't forewarn you more than a few days sooner that I was bringing two guests. Maybe we can house Veronica in the spare upstairs bedroom. Right now I am going to see George in the scrap yard and bring him back to the house to see his mother."

Wanda left the house and walked toward the scrap yard. There had been more roads added to the network where the scrap iron was being stacked waiting to be torn apart, cutup, or smashed apart. Mildred quickly caught up to Wanda, as she had something important to tell her.

"Wanda, hold on a minute. You do not know this, and you may or may not like what I am about to tell you. Your friend Jill has been going out with George while you were gone."

"Oh really," Wanda replied with a surprised and somewhat disappointed look. "When did this all take place?

"It started when Jill invited him to the party to cap off her history class on Japan. They went on dates on most the Saturday nights when you were gone. They have been sitting together on Sundays at church. Keep in mind that for the past two years you have rejected George at almost every turn."

"You know, you are right. I don't blame Jill and George," Wanda responded.

They were now at where George was working in the scrap yard. It was time for Wanda to talk to George. Wanda walked slowly up behind George in an attempt to scare him. "George," she shouted!

"Wanda, you're back! It is good to have you back." George looked at Wanda and noticed that her physical size had not changed much since she left. She noticed that he was observing her and figured that he had probably noticed that she had not gone through with the abortion she had planned to have.

Chapter 9

"George, I have two pieces of good news for you." He put down the cutting torch and sat down on a Model T front seat and invited Wanda to join him.

"Wanda, please sit down on this seat with me. You have some good news. What? The war is over? The price of scrap iron is up?"

"No," answered Wanda. "I saw your family."

"That is great," replied George, "and how are they?"

"They are all fine," answered Wanda. "Now, for the really good news. You have a new little baby sister." George was very quiet for a few seconds.

"Say that again Wanda, please."

"You have a little baby sister born in Stockton, California just 6 days ago. Both your baby sister and your mother are sitting with Mildred drinking coffee in our kitchen."

"You are kidding. Really? I did not know that she was with child."

"Yes, really George." George quickly jumped up and began to run toward the house. Then he stopped as quickly as he took off.

"I'm sorry, I need to wait for you." He ran back, took Wanda's hand, and began to walk with her. "I really did miss you, Wanda."

On their way back to the house, they held hands. This was the first time this had happened since George came to Harriet. He noticed that she was a little nicer to him and even squeezed his hand.

When they arrived at the house, George and his mother hugged each other and both sat on the couch. George then held his new baby sister.

"So, Mom, what is little sister's name?" he asked.

"Her name is Angelina Wanda, after your girlfriend," George's mother answered. Wanda looked at the little baby and then at George. It was the first time anyone had referred to Wanda as George's girlfriend in front of him. It was an awkward moment for everyone in the room except George's mother. No one knew what to say, especially Wanda.

The Olson's invitation to George's mother to stay a week, along with the strings pulled by Felix Mitchell, the government official, was enough for Mrs. Robinson to be granted permission to remain in Harriet to heal completely and to rest up. During the week Mrs. Robinson was a guest speaker at the Olson's church. A number of people from other churches attended to hear what she had to say about the country that the United States was at war with. Many in Harriet wanted to hear what the common people were like in Japan. Most of the people in the United States had the idea that it was the Japanese government only that was mostly in favor of the war. Mrs. Robinson confirmed that fact.

As soon as his mother and baby Angelina Wanda had arrived at the Olson home, George fell in love with the little baby. Wanda started going to school once again and spent very little time with the baby she helped to deliver. George took care of the little baby whenever he had the opportunity, usually after the evening meal.

Chapter 9

One of the items that came in as surplus was a beautiful baby buggy. George washed it up and oiled the wheels. He also found some beautiful blankets that Mildred washed for him. George was able to give Angelina Wanda rides around the scrapyard roads, during which she would most often fall asleep.

George's mother could plainly see that he was becoming very much attached to this little girl. It was not much of a stretch for her to imagine that Wanda and George could very easily solve Wanda's dilemma if the two would get married.

Wanda started working with a social service to find a suitable set of parents for her baby, although she had not yet completely decided to give her baby up. She interviewed three couples from other towns that were judged to be good parents. She had earlier eliminated another of her options—that of abortion. Wanda did not tell anyone of this decision, although many suspected it.

George wanted so much to have a relationship with Wanda. She knew that he had an itch for her. He was sure that her choice of male companionship was not what God wanted for her. George prayed at the dinner table one noon when Wanda was at class some 50 miles away. Mr. and Mrs. Olson were present at the table, along with Georges's mother.

"Lord, we need to ask you for your help with Wanda. As you are aware, she is thinking about giving away that beautiful life growing inside of her to a couple who desire a child but cannot have one. I believe that would be your second choice for Wanda. Mildred and Thomas are of the same opinion. Lord, it could be that this may be their only chance to be a Grandma and Grandpa.

Please do several things: Protect that little one inside of Wanda, keep both of them healthy, cause her to think of the welfare of her baby, and cause her to want to keep and raise it. Cause something to happen so she will want to be a mother. Wanda will need a good husband and daddy to that little baby. We have our own opinion of who that person could be and you know who I am speaking of. It's up to you Lord.—Amen.

"Thank you for that prayer," Mildred said "it is just how we have been praying."

George needed to make a trip to Madison, Wisconsin to attend some business concerning the government scrap salvage program. There were some of the midsize communities in the state who were having some difficulty with storing and making disposition of the

Chapter 9

massive amount of contributions made to the scrap salvage program. He would be gone for only 3 days.

He needed Wanda to help Mrs. Robinson take care of little Angelina. The baby was getting stronger and the mother was also on her way to full recovery. It wouldn't be long and his mother would be going back to California

The next day George asked Wanda to meet him in the apple orchard a short walk from the house. She had just come home from school on the bus for the weekend. There were two swings hanging from a branch on a big oak tree. "Wanda, I need to leave the scrap yard for a few days. I would like you to help my mother take care of little Angelina when I am gone. Mother is still not feeling as well as she should be. She really needs rest. Little Angelina thinks that I am her daddy. You be her daddy while I am gone."

"I will do my best," Wanda answered, "although I hope you won't be gone too long. I've seen how you are attracted to her and how well she responds to you. You will make a great daddy someday."

"Wanda, I would like to propose something to you. Please do not comment until you've had a chance to think about what I am going to propose."

"George, go ahead and tell me what you have on your mind." She was thinking that this proposal had something to do with taking care of little Angelina, although another kind of proposal had crossed her mind.

'Wanda, I really want you to find a husband and get married. Then you should have your baby and keep it. You will make a great mother. You would make your mom and dad the happiest people in the world."

"George, you are one of the nicest guys that I have ever met. However, the one thing I have learned from my parents about marriage—you need to be in love with the one you marry. I don't even have a boyfriend at this point."

"What about your friend Bruce?" George said.

"My girlfriends told me that Bruce says that he does not want me," Wanda replied.

"Has he given a reason?" George asked.

"He has told some of his friends that he believes that my baby will be born with a disease of some type, because the fathers are tramps and have slept in places inhabited by rodents." At this point Wanda began to weep. George did not know how to handle this. They both sat in the swings for the next 5 minutes until Wanda regained her composure. Finally, George gently patted Wanda on the back of her neck.

"Wanda, listen, I feel so strongly about this that if you cannot find someone to marry, I will marry you."

"But I do not love you in the way that two people getting married should be in love. You're a nice guy, but that is as far as it goes. For over two years I have rejected you while you have been so nice to me."

"Well, let me ask you a question," George responded.

"Shoot," Wanda replied.

"Which is the more important, to marry the one you love, or to love the one you marry?"

Chapter 9

"Probably, the former." Wanda was sure she had the correct answer. "What do you think, George?"

"Actually, if the truth be known, both are important. But, let me tell you about my parents. When they met in Japan, my mother was a missionary and a Christian. My father was not a Christian and fell in love with my mom, the missionary. He would attend the camp where she was a nurse and would attend some of the meetings and listen to her speak—both in English and in Japanese."

"Couldn't they just get married and try to work it out?" Wanda inquired.

"Actually, my dad asked my mom that exact same question."

"What did she answer?" Wanda asked. George sensed that she was becoming more interested in this subject.

"She told my dad what the Bible says on this subject. The bible says, 'Be thou not unequally yoked'. This means that it's like a cow being yoked with a horse. The team would be useless to a farmer. The two animals would maybe walk down the field together, but would they get much done in harmony? Of Course Not!!" Wanda looked at George and knew he was correct in what he was saying.

"So what happened to cause them to marry?" She was curious, just what George wanted.

"One night my mom convinced him through her talk that he needed to convert to Christianity. That night before he fell asleep, he did just that, only he never told her. My dad came to see her every night after that. She noticed the change in his personality, his attitude toward her and her work. He became more interested in what she was doing. His own religion had been empty. Two weeks later, he asked her again to marry him. He was surprised when she answered yes."

"But," Wanda said, "She wasn't in love with him."

"That is true, and she knew that and told him as much. She told him that now that they were equally yoked spiritually, she would learn to love him and it didn't take long." Wanda was quiet for the next few moments while she contemplated what George had just said. "Wanda, please think about my proposal during the time that I am gone. I believe that you and I are on the same wave length, spiritually. We would just need to fall in love with each other, of which 50% of that process is already accomplished on my part."

With that, George got up from his swing seat, stepped over in front of Wanda, took her hand, kissed it, and said "Good bye, Wanda."

Chapter 10

Wanda's best friend, Jill, had not had a chance to chat with Wanda since she returned from her trip to California. She wanted to tell her about her dates with George and explain that her intention was not necessarily romantic, although it could have easily grown into that. She walked over to the Olson residence and knocked at the door. "Wanda," Jill said as Wanda opened the front door. "You are back. Did you have an eventful trip?"

"Yes I am back, and I had a chance to think about my entire situation. You and I need to talk." Jill immediately thought that Wanda was planning on dumping on her for stealing her boyfriend.

Jill interrupted—"Let me talk first. I had several so called dates with George when you were gone. I needed someone to go with me to a church function. It started out like that. I could see that George was a better person when he had a companion, which you apparently never provided him with."

"Jill, say no more," Wanda replied almost immediately, "I now want to be his only companion. I am falling in love with him. You are partly the cause of that. Thank you. Does that surprise you? Let me make some coffee inside and we will talk."

Jill walked inside and sat down on the couch while Wanda went to the kitchen and began making coffee. When it was done, she brought 2 cups of hot coffee into the living room and set them on the coffee table in front of the couch.

"So, Wanda, what happened out in California?" Jill asked.

"Several things took place, which I will tell you about, but first you need to know that I have changed my whole thinking on the situation I got myself into. When I took off for the west coast, my intentions were all upside down. As I met various people, my thinking gradually got straightened around. Then I met George's mother and dad. Then I helped deliver their little baby—George's sister. That was a real joy.

"I talked to a girl who had experienced an abortion. That and a tour of an abortion mill convinced me to cross that option off my list of alternative solutions. Those two experiences plus visiting with George's family made the entire trip worthwhile."

Suddenly George's little sister woke up in the bedroom and started crying. "Jill, walk into the bedroom and pick up George's little sister and bring her in here." Very quickly, Jill was back and carrying little Angelina Wanda. She gradually stopped crying. Wanda and Jill continued their discussion about the trip to California for the next half hour until it was time for Jill to leave. When Jill set the baby down and walked out of the house Angelina started crying once again.

Wanda immediately took the crying baby from off the sofa and started feeding her a bottle of mother's milk. The baby soon fell back to sleep. Wanda felt very good about herself as Angelina apparently felt comfortable in her arms and drank all her bottle of milk. "It appears that you are a natural for feeding a baby, Wanda," Mildred commented as they both sat down at the kitchen table to drink a

Chapter 10

cup of coffee. "The baby senses that her mother is not feeling well and cries."

"That is the first time I have held Angelina and have given her a bottle at the same time," she replied. "When I was at my nursing job at the hospital I took care of a couple of mothers with babies. But they were both nursing mothers."

"Let me ask you a question Wanda," Mildred asked. "If you were going to keep your baby, how would you feed—by nursing or by a bottle?"

"It would all depend on if my body was able to produce a sufficient amount of milk. My first choice would be to feed by breast-feeding," she responded.

That night George's mother decided that she needed to return to her husband and family in California. She had a return trip ticket. It was time.

The next day Mildred took her to the Harriet train depot. Wanda went along, carrying Angelina. She hated to give up the little tyke and cried when she handed Angelina over to her mother. As they were driving back home Wanda commented to her mother, "Maybe I shouldn't give up my baby."

"That would be a very wise decision, Wanda," Mildred said. It would make your mom and dad very happy, and it would be a happy ending to a tragedy. Only one additional thing would make it happier."

George reached Madison later in the afternoon. When he arrived at the bus depot there were three federal policeman that immediately surrounded him. "Mr. Robinson, come with us, you are under arrest."

"Exactly what am I being arrested for?" George questioned sharply.

"For evading the Japanese internment program in 1942. You will need to take a bus back to California under guard."

"There must be some mistake," George retorted. "You need to contact Fred Wilcox in Harriet, Wisconsin. Apparently, the right hand doesn't know what the left hand is doing." George decided not to resist what the three officers were attempting to do. It would only make the situation worse.

George was soon handcuffed and on another bus on his way to Stockton, California. Before he left he had the officers promise to notify the Olsons back in Harriet about the arrest and where he was headed. They promised that they would at least do that for him. George gave them the Olson's phone number in Harriet.

The next trip to Dr. Thysell's office by Wanda revealed that there were some problems with the development of the baby inside of her. It was a rare condition probably caused by the damage done to her body during the rape attack. Only an operation on the baby while still inside the mother would possibly solve the problem. The doctor said that no surgeon in the world had ever performed such a procedure, at least he had never heard of one.

Wanda decided to temporarily stop her college studies because of this physical condition. The doctors also told her that she had best stay close to the hospital in case an emergency should occur. For a

Chapter 10

while she was able to do some of her school work from home. It wasn't long before she lost all interest in school. She decided finally to put her schooling on hold.

Word had gotten back to the Olson's and Wanda that George was in an internment camp in California. Thomas immediately informed Mr. Wilcox about this development and Felix began an investigation to find out where the system broke down.

Meanwhile, Wanda had written to George at the internment camp and informed him about her and the baby's medical problem. "The doctor says that they need a specialist to operate on the baby while it is inside me if the baby is to be completely normal when born," she wrote. "This will need to be done as soon as possible. Everyone is praying for me. Please do likewise. Also, for your information, I have decided to keep the baby and raise it myself." George was glad to hear this news about Wanda's change of direction, except for the medical condition. That was not good news. *She needs to get married, also,* he thought.

George became acquainted once again with his family at the internment camp. He also met other Japanese people who had been sent to the camp since he had left Los Angeles in 1942. Many of these newcomers were from colleges and universities.

One of these people was a baby neonatal research specialist from a medical school in Oregon. His name was Dr. Yuu Toyy and he was highly recommended and praised by the Japanese community at the internment camp. George began talking to him about Wanda's medical problem. "She has one of the medical conditions that is in my field of expertise and research," he said to George. "It sounds just like one of my cases two years ago."

"Would you be willing to take a train out to Wisconsin and talk to Wanda and her doctor?" George asked the Japanese doctor. "I would need to get you out there—exactly how, I do not know. I do not think it would be safe to bring Wanda here because of her current medical condition."

"Yes, but how in the world would I get there without getting into further trouble? I have some money, but I cannot get at it. It's at a bank in Eugene, Oregon. Do you have some option whereby I could get there? And would they let me out of here to make the trip?'

Meanwhile, George became friends with some of the guards at the internment camp. Many of them had a very one-sided feeling of what the U.S. Government was doing with the Japanese families. Most of them felt that it was wrong and a mistake to intern the Japanese without a just cause—but what could they do about it? George decided to take a chance on planning an escape for the doctor and himself on the railroad where he had ridden when he first went to Harriet. He organized a group that would help plan the escape. He explained and promised that he would go to prison for all of the group if anyone got caught. In this group were 2 American guards, the Japanese doctor, a Japanese lawyer from Los Angeles, and George. They had two meetings out in the middle of the big court area where many of the Japanese met often. They needed to meet in a place where their voices could not be monitored or recorded.

In the first meeting George explained how he and the Japanese doctor would hop the freight train and ride to Harriet, Wisconsin. The second meeting, they discussed how they might escape from the internment camp without being caught. This would be difficult unless one of the group came up with an ingenious escape plan.

Chapter 10

George went to the camp library and found some railroad maps of California and the U.S. He redrew them into a notebook and studied them until he had them memorized.

The two guards broke into the main guard shack and modified the schedule so that no one was scheduled to guard the main entrance on Sunday at 8 p.m. They left a 10 minute window.

George and the doctor escaped and dressed in some tramp-looking clothes suitable for a boxcar ride. They walked to the set of tracks where a slow moving freight was scheduled. The two guards had set the alarm so that it was silent while the two escapees went through the gate between 7:45 and 8 p.m. It would be the next morning before the camp director would be notified of the missing inmates.

Dr. Toyy was a little hesitant to jump on a freight. It was rarely done in Japan or by Japanese people in America.

George and the Doctor both climbed on and rode until the long train stopped to let the steam engines take on water and coal. It was a junction where three railroads met. They jumped off and waited for a slow moving freight to appear on the track where George had indicated on his map. He then found an open boxcar to ride in. He had his map and kept referring to it whenever the train passed a mile sign post.

Within only two hours they were at the spot where the train would pass on its way to the east coast rail line. They had packed a sufficient lunch to hold them until they would expect to arrive in Harriet.

Both of them brought a small pillow to rest their heads on in the boxcar. They were fortunate in riding in a car that had some well-behaved individuals. They were not loud, drunk, or drinking. Also, there were no women on the boxcar to tempt the men.

It took the two "Hobos" 4 days to make the trip from California to Wisconsin. During the trip the two got caught up on the war news, the political situation in both warring countries, and their families.

After many hours of rough riding and growling stomachs, George saw the Harriet signpost and prepared to jump off the boxcar. They exited the freight train at 4 a.m. at the same spot where George exited the train before. George was afraid that the authorities would find the doctor if they found him. He needed to make his way back to the internment camp to protect everyone involved with their escape to Harriet.

The train was traveling much faster that George thought safe, but he gave Dr. Toyy a quick lesson on how to land. He had learned it from some of the other hoboes on his other trip. The weeds happened to be thick and high and the doctor kept his arms and hands close to his body so as not to injure them. They were the most valuable tools he had for operating. George prayed a quick prayer for Dr. Toyy.

When they arrived at the Olson home, George woke up Thomas at 5 a.m. and introduced him to the Japanese doctor. "Mr. Olson, please introduce Dr. Toyy to Doc Thysell tomorrow morning along with Wanda. He will see if he can operate on her baby. I will be on my way back to California to shield the escape team from arrest and prosecution."

"Dr. Toyy, can you do me a favor?"

"I will, George," the doctor responded.

"Pease tell Wanda that I may not see her for a while. I suspect that they will throw me in a California prison."

Chapter 10

"I will do that for you, George," the doctor said. "Tell me, is she your girlfriend?"

"I don't know if she will still have me. God will need to determine what happens there."

George then found another freight train going to the west coast. This one was going faster than what was the recommended speed for hoping a freight. But he was lucky. Once he grabbed ahold of the boxcar ladder, the freight quickly slowed down to what the safe boxcar hopping speed limit was.

It would take him a week to arrive back at the camp. He needed to return to the internment camp to assume the guilt for his escape, the Japanese doctor's escape, and the involvement of the 2 guards in the break. The lawyer's involvement was in case legal advice was needed. He would be needed to plead for George to assume the punishment for the entire group.

When Wanda arrived at the breakfast table at 7 a.m. she was surprised to find the Japanese doctor sitting where George usually sat. He was drinking coffee. Mildred was the first to speak. "Wanda, I want to introduce you to the doctor who would like to talk to you about your medical problem. He is a miracle sent from God and George and will be able to operate on your baby. That's if you approve." They both shook hands with each other. Wanda wasn't sure what it was all about. She needed some explanation.

"So, Mother, how did this all come about?"

"I really don't know. I guess the doctor and George came in on the morning freight. They met in an internment camp in California."

"George was here this morning?" Wanda asked with surprise and a sudden excitement.

"That is what your father said," Mildred responded. The doctor sensed that the mother and daughter were in the dark. He needed to inform them how his appearance came about.

"Let me explain," the doctor interjected. "George was sent back to the internment camp about two weeks ago. I just arrived at the camp myself about a month ago. We happened to meet at an afternoon coffee session. I happened to tell him what my field of study is at the college where I teach. He told me about his girlfriend having a baby inside of her that has a condition that needs to be operated on. I have never performed a procedure of this kind and neither has any other doctor. However, I have done research on these kind of cases. If we could operate so that the baby's growth could be normal, then the baby would not be crippled when born."

Wanda and Mildred sat listening intently as the doctor continued explaining the procedure that would be necessary if the baby was to be born normally. The mother-to-be and grandmother-to-be seemed to grasp the delicate operation that was being explained.

Back in the internment camp, George and his family were praying that the doctor would convince Wanda to choose to have doctor Toyy perform the operation.

Chapter 10

"Wanda," the Japanese doctor began to say, "What I would like you to do is to talk to your doctor and see if he will meet with us and let me explain what I would propose to do. I will need to have a special setup to perform the operation and to have his and your permission. One thing I do not want is the media to plaster the operation all over the press. Then the government will come and get me with guns, and force me to tell where George is."

"Let's do it doc," Wanda answered, "I now agree that this will be a very special baby," Wanda told everyone present. Wanda seemed to trust the doctor in the manner that he spoke.

The Japanese doctor and Wanda's personal doctor decided to work together to insure that everything would go smoothly. Some additional instrumentation was needed. Some of the equipment needed was to be shipped from Dr. Toyy's laboratory in Oregon. The doctor was able to accomplish this using one of his colleagues at the university where he taught. The equipment would be shipped directly to the Harriet Hospital from Dr. Toyy's college offce.

Wanda asked doctor Toyy when George would be coming back. "I am not sure if he will be returning any time soon," the doctor told her.

"And why not?" Wanda asked.

"George offered to take the rap for the entire string of broken laws and the people who broke them," the doctor explained. "He just wanted for you to have a normal birth, with a healthy baby."

"Did he ever refer to me as his girlfriend?" she asked.

"He referred to you as a very special friend," the doctor said. He then delivered his opinion to Wanda on what would probably happen to George. "It would be my guess that George will spend some time in the state prison." Wanda became very quiet.

Wanda had a lot of thinking to do. She walked to the swing in back of the house. Her longtime boyfriend, Bruce, was not interested in marrying her. He added insult to his turndown by telling Jill that raising a crippled child was "not for me." She thought about George's desire to help raise the baby. "He also hinted at wanting to marry me," she said to herself as she made another push on the swing.

At that point, Wanda made a decision. She bowed her head and began to pray. *"Lord, I want you to cause me to fall in love with George. Keep him safe in the internment camp. Provide a release time for him as soon as possible so he will be freed. Keep your hand on the baby inside me. Forgive me for all of my doubt and mistrust in your will for my life. Guide the hands of the doctor that will operate on us—the baby and Me.—Amen*

As she opened her eyes a calmness came over her whole body. She got up from the swing and walked back to the house and to the kitchen table. There she sat down with her mother and dad. "I have something important to tell you two. You might want to let me get you a fresh cup of coffee before I began." Wanda poured a fresh cup of coffee for each of them. When they were all settled, Wanda began to talk.

"I just prayed that God would cause me to fall in love with George. That may be a surprise to you."

Chapter 10

"We have news for you, my dear. You are already in love with George," Mildred announced.

"How do you figure that, Mother?" Wanda asked.

"Well, let's see. You've showed your concern for him on several occasions."

"When, and for what?" Wanda asked.

"When he burned his foot—when you looked at it the second time," Mildred responded. "When you've brought lunch out to him at the scrap pile on several occasions. When you needed help with your algebra. Several times you would ask me where George is, when you came home from school. Now that he is not here, you are concerned about him. Do you need any additional proof that you have an itch for George?"

"I guess not Mom. Now I'm worried that he won't be back here soon—or at all."

"Well, don't you think you should write to him and tell him that you want him back in Harriet?" Mildred said. "Tell him that you need him when your baby is operated on and when the baby is born. Tell him that you need a husband and your baby needs a daddy."

"If he will still have me," Wanda replied. "He thinks I don't love him. At least that is the last word he got from me."

Wanda immediately sat down and wrote a long letter to George which he received in 3 days.

George received the letter and was pleasantly surprised. He immediately brought the letter to the Internment Camp Commandant and explained the entire story to him. He was very understanding but told George that he was sorry but George would need to do the time in the state prison. "What you did George was to break laws and camp rules and you organized a camp escape. You will need to be in our prison system for at least a few more months. Maybe I can find a judge that will provide some clemency. Maybe I can set up a session where you can explain your entire story to him."

It was on a Tuesday that Dr. Toyy was scheduled to operate on the baby inside of Wanda. She was 7 months along in her pregnancy and the operation could not be delayed beyond that time. The two doctors met at the Harriet Hospital in a specially equipped surgical room. Dr. Toyy met with the nurses ahead of time and went through the entire procedure to be done.

The operation would take two hours, if everything went according to what was planned by Dr. Toyy. It would take a full week of rest for Wanda to heal. The doctor decided to stay in Harriet and not return to the internment camp. He would return to the west coast when he could safely return to the college where he taught. He would closely monitor Wanda's condition in the event there was any change in her condition. He also wanted to document the entire operation for further research for when he returned to his college. Dr. Toyy was also interested in performing the same operation some day in the future if it could be used to save a baby's life.

Chapter 10

The operation on Wanda and the baby went smoothly without any complications. Wanda was awake and conscious during the entire operation. It was as if God Himself was placed in the doctor's hands.

April 15, 1945

It was Sunday morning when Wanda called out for her mother at about 5 a.m. "Mom, you better come here! You're going to have to help me." Mildred hurried into Wanda's bedroom and immediately noticed that she was having labor pains. The family did not wish to take any chances delivering the baby at home so they quickly got into the car and drove to the hospital. Thomas called both doctors and asked them to meet at the hospital.

The delivery went smoothly with no hitches. A little daughter was born to Wanda. Doctor Thysell and Dr. Toyy both examined the little girl and they determined that she was perfect. They kept the baby in the hospital an extra 3 days to make certain everything remained well. Wanda also stayed at the hospital to help take care of the baby.

When Wanda and the baby arrived home, Maxine, the guard dog became aware that a stranger had entered the territory, but this stranger was special. She barked until the baby begin to whimper—then she stopped. Wanda sensed that the dog somehow understood that the new arrival was part of Wanda. Once she introduced Maxine to the new baby, the puppy laid down on the floor next to wherever the baby was set—the couch, the crib, the bed, in someone's lap, etc.

Wanda and Mildred started to divide the downstairs bedroom into a nursery. They also spent time searching for baby clothes from the piles of surplus baby clothes for boys and girls that had been collected in the surplus program. There was also nice baby furniture that had been collected during the war surplus collection months. Mrs. Olson had set some of these aside to sell when the war was over. A few items of furniture were placed in the baby's nursery.

Wanda received only two letters from George and then they stopped. She had no idea why. Maybe the prison where he was being held did not allow communications between the Japanese and the outside World. She continued to write just in case the prison authorities never handed Wanda's letters to him. Maybe he received her letters but they never sent his letters.

She began to wonder if she would have to travel to the prison to see him. She began to pray for his safe return.

While most of the Japanese-Americans were soon out of the internment camps after the war, George was transferred to the state prison for a few months longer.

He was let out on July 1, 1945. He went to his home in Los Angeles where his family had lived before the war. He had not received any communications from his family or from anyone in Harriet. The mail system apparently broke down involving the internment camps, at least the one that George was in.

When he was done visiting at his former home, he decided to save the money and bum a freight to Harriet to start work again with his adopted family. He wondered what happened to Wanda's baby — what

Chapter 10

was her decision about keeping the baby? Was the operation successful? Did she marry anyone? If he returned to Harriet would he upset the family dynamics? Many questions entered his mind as he waited for an open boxcar on a relatively slow moving freight.

He found the same freight as he had taken twice before. This time the ride was much quieter. It had been raining and it was colder than expected. George had kept his ear to the weather forecast and was ready for it. He brought a t-shirt he had picked up at the prison goodwill store where the inmates could buy various items that they needed and could afford to buy with the little money they earned by working.

He got settled in and fell asleep in one corner of a boxcar that apparently had been used for hauling hay from the Midwest and was returning back probably to get more hay. It was a good smell reminding him of the aroma from the fields close to the Wisconsin farms.

He begin to dream of what he would find when he returned to Harriet. It was an awful dream. He dreamt that when he returned, he no longer had a job in the scrap yard, Wanda had her baby and had given it away. The profitability of the scrap business had gone way south and Wanda was no longer available. She had found a doctoral student for a boyfriend. George finally woke up. The train had stopped, the sun had come out, and George was hungry. He quickly packed up and jumped off.

He walked for 3 blocks and spotted a Japanese restaurant sign. Was that by chance or by divine design? He walked in and sat down at a booth. A man walked over to his booth and greeted George. "What can I get you sir?"

"Hello, this is a lovely day, isn't it?" George spoke to the person whom he assumed was the owner.

"It is indeed a lovely day," the man answered, whom George recognized right away as being Japanese—all Japanese.

"I would like something Japanese—anything Japanese," George answered.

"I have been closed for almost 3 years due to being in an internment camp," the owner said.

"Which camp?" George asked.

"The one near Stockton, California," the owner answered. The two men exchanged comments concerning the facility that both had been in for a while. Soon George received his food. It was the first time he had eaten authentic Japanese food since shortly before his leaving home in 1942.

George soon found another freight and hopped on. As he rode the slow moving freights across the west and then the mid-west, there were still some of the same old boys riding the boxcars. This time George was ready for them in case they got out of hand. In 3 years he had grown another 2 inches and gained at least 40 pounds—all muscles from handling scrap iron.

George arrived in Harriet at 5 a.m. in the morning. He got a ride from the town policeman, Ray Alm. Expecting everyone to be asleep at the Olson house, he quietly sat down on the porch. He happened to look in the window where he saw that a woman was sitting in a rocking chair with a baby asleep in her lap. The baby was dressed in pink and had a cute bonnet on her head. The outside street light was reflecting off of the women's face. He looked closer and saw that the woman was Wanda and he assumed the baby was her new born.

Chapter 10

That meant that Wanda had her baby, the Japanese doctor's operation was successful, and Mama and daughter were together. *I wonder who she married or if she married?* He thought to himself. *Maybe I should have not made an appearance until I made sure that Wanda was not married. I will risk it,* he again thought to himself.

There was a rocking chair on the porch. George sat down in the chair and began to rock. It soon begin to make a constant repetitive creaking sound. Wanda was awakened by the noise and listened intently. She stood up taking care not to wake her little girl. She walked to the screen door and looked out. She saw George sitting and rocking. They looked at each other for at least 30 seconds. Three years of thoughts passed through their minds in that half minute. Then she slowly opened the screen door taking care as not to awaken the baby.

Wanda carefully set the baby in George's arms and he continued to rock. Then Wanda quietly disappeared back into the house. For the next 5 minutes George rocked Wanda's daughter and had a feeling of jubilation rushing through his body. Soon George heard the noise of people getting out of bed and descending down from upstairs to the screen door. The baby was still asleep as they all passed through the front door.

"Wanda, what did you name her?" George asked.

"Mary Barbara Robinson," Wanda responded. George stopped rocking all of a sudden. He stared at the train that had just stopped on the Chicago and Northwestern Railroad track. "Do you know what that means, George?"

"What," George answered.

"It means that you and I need to get married today," Wanda responded. "You will then fulfill your promise to me."

"And I will need to make a trip to the courthouse to adopt little Mary," George answered. "Can we take care of both at the same time?"

"You bet we can," Wanda answered.

Because of the expected publicity if a big wedding was held, Wanda and George decided to have a private wedding in the Olson living room. Pastor Williams performed the ceremony with Jill Miller singing a couple of songs, and with a light lunch served. The Harriett Press got wind of the quickly planned wedding and wanted to make it a major event. The couple said that several persons may be in danger of being harassed by reporters from many newspapers. The Press withdrew the request.

Wanda continued with her education while George continued expanding the scrap and fur business with Thomas and Mildred.

God continued to bless George, Wanda, and Mary Barbara.

The End

CPSIA information can be obtained
at www.ICGtesting.com
Printed in the USA
FSOW04n0013070716
22430FS

9 781498 478199